W0007705

Carlo Fruttero and Franco Lucentini were a well-known literary duo in Italy for several decades until Lucentini's death in 2002. For about forty years they co-wrote newspaper and magazine articles, literary essays, edited numerous anthologies and published six ground-breaking and best-selling mystery novels. Their first novel, *The Sunday Woman*, was made into a film in 1975 starring Marcello Mastroianni, Jacqueline Bisset and Jean-Louis Trintignant. *Runaway Horses* and *The Lover of No Fixed Abode* were translated by Gregory Dowling and first published in English by Bitter Lemon Press.

RUNAWAY HORSES

Carlo Fruttero
and
Franco Lucentini

Translated by
Gregory Dowling

BITTER LEMON PRESS
LONDON

BITTER LEMON PRESS

First published in the United Kingdom in 2025 by
Bitter Lemon Press, 47 Wilmington Square, London WC1X OET
www.bitterlemonpress.com

First published in Italian in 1983 as *Il palio delle contrade morte* by
Arnoldo Mondadori Editore S.p.A., Milano
© 1983 Arnoldo Mondadori Editore S.p.A., Milano
© 2019 Mondadori Libri S.p.A., Milano
English translation © 2025 Gregory Dowling

This Work has been translated with the contribution of Centro per
il libro e la lettura del Ministero della Cultura Italiano.

CENTRO
PER IL LIBRO
E LA LETTURA

A CIP record for this book is available from the British Library

PB ISBN 978–1–916725–034
eBook USC ISBN 978–1–916725–041
eBook ROW ISBN 978–1–916725–058

Typeset by Tetragon, London
Printed and bound by the CPI Group (UK) Ltd, Croydon, CRO 4YY

CONTENTS

The authors thank Lorenzo and Titti Nepi
and Vittoria Bonelli Zondadari for their valuable advice.

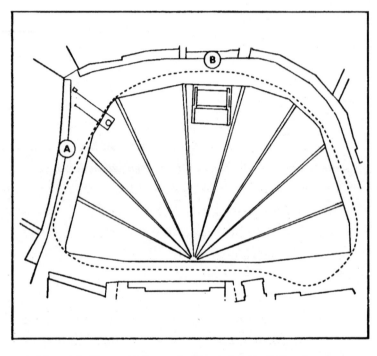

*Map of the Piazza del Campo in Siena where the Palio takes place,
with the optimal route of the horses indicated by the dotted line.*

*The two circles indicate the position of Avvocato
Maggioni (A) and that of his wife Valeria (B).*

I

Avvocato Maggioni has been looking out of this window for a good half hour by now, and beneath him the procession that precedes the Siena Palio horse race continues to parade by very slowly.

The gently curved polygon of the Piazza del Campo blazes with a dazzling variety of colours, from the vivid tinctures of the banners to the pale ochres of the palazzi and the dizzying pointillism of the crowd, whose components are hemmed in by the ring of earth around which the race will be run or, like the lawyer, are leaning out of windows, balconies, podiums, merlons and garrets to contemplate the sumptuous serpent of the procession as it inches forward, halts, then moves again to the shrill sound of an endlessly repeated marching tune.

In the medieval costumes of the different *contrade* the lawyer keeps finding new shades and unexpected combinations among the bright or ashy blues, the purples and golds, the shy or resolute greens, the yellows, whites and blacks, whose tones are forever being retouched by the flickering alternation of sunlight and shade. And he misses none of the shimmering splendours of the velvets, silks and brocades, the dull hues of boots, harnesses and jerkins, the intermittent gleams of cuirasses, crests, spurs and halberds.

Spectacular multiplicity. Captivating vision.

But Maggioni is not here to admire. He is not here, let's be frank, to enjoy himself. Rather, his eyes are surveying the scene; they are scrutinizing it.

Until the other day he knew practically nothing about the Palio, neither had he ever seen one. He had been in Siena perhaps three times in his life and never around 16 August (or 2 July). The Palio was for him just another of those folkloristic events that take place in so many cities, consisting of ten per cent tradition (more or less spurious) and ninety per cent tourism; he would never have imagined that his wife Valeria and he might end up involved in it. To what extent, in exactly what way, he doesn't yet know. But he has some clues, some strong suspicions.

Below his window the *contrada* of the Eagle has now halted. The drums roll, the yellow-gold banners, with the double-headed black eagle, soar high into the air, hover for an instant, fold in on themselves and drop back into the firm grips of the standard-bearers. There is a roar of applause, while more distant roars, at intervals along the parade route, acclaim the aerial feats of other gaudy standards.

The older American woman to his right offers him her binoculars with a smile. Earlier it was he who had asked to borrow them, and ever since, at regular intervals, she has pressed them on him.

The lawyer removes his left arm from Ginevra's shoulders as she stands there with her elbows on the sill, her long blonde hair tumbling down towards the piazza as if to invite a lover to climb up. He adjusts the focus.

He at once zeroes in on his wife, over there, on the balcony of the Circolo degli Uniti, the Circle of the United. Valeria is frenziedly applauding the exhibition of the standard-bearers of the Wave, in white and blue. In three days, no, just two, the Wave has become her *contrada*. Wild enthusiasm, visceral participation, which initially of course amazed and irritated him. A woman like her, well balanced and full of housewifely discretion, going crazy over something that in no way concerns her, that she knows nothing at all about? I mean, seriously?

Poor Valeria, who now turns flirtatiously to the extremely handsome (so she thinks) man beside her. Blue shirt and cravat (Gucci?), noble forehead with yachtsman's tan, hair tinged with grey, aquiline nose, gleaming teeth. His name is Guidobaldo. He is a count. He has lands and castles hereabouts.

Valeria is smiling up at him (the count is of course very tall), fluttering her eyelashes (he must have convinced her that she has marvellous eyes). She says something with (he could bet on it) that new throaty voice of hers, which no one had ever heard her use until three days ago. He hands her a packet of Marlboro cigarettes with those long, strong fingers, and flicks a flame from a gold lighter (Cartier?).

Key moment from a TV ad, thinks Avvocato Maggioni. And the scene, bordering on the artificial, the constructed, the rigged, confirms certain suspicions and apprehensions that no longer have (or never did have) anything to do with jealousy. He lowers the angle of the binoculars, and on the edge of the racetrack a muscular attendant in jeans enters the scene, swigging from a bottle of Pepsi. There you go, thinks the lawyer, there you go.

He hands the binoculars back to the American woman, forcing a broad smile onto his face, and puts his arm around Ginevra's shoulders again; she straightens up, rubs her head and side against him like a young animal (a filly? a fawn? who can say?). Her hair, which is too blonde, too soft, gives off a perfume that is undefinable but can certainly be classified as provocative, at least to a middle-aged professional man. Is it the shampoo she uses? Or her eau de toilette? Or maybe a soap, a deodorant.

The lawyer kisses her on the neck, in any case (is that what she wants from him?), and reckons that right now he is being just as soppy and sickening as Valeria, over there with her count. Just as implausible.

Below the Torre del Mangia the band of trumpets and drums resumes its rudimentary marching tune, the *contrada* of the Eagle moves off at a rhythmical tramp, first the standard-bearers with the drummer, then the leader and the men-at-arms, then the principal pageboy with the big banner and all the other pageboys, the jockey in ceremonial gear on the parade horse led by the groom, the "*bàrbero*", bringing up the rear, while, with the same deliberate slowness, the *contrada* of the Porcupine moves forward in the same order, white with red, black and blue arabesques...

Lively, triumphant colours everywhere, before the lawyer's eyes. But he cannot accept this magnificent chromatic exaltation, this prodigious theatrical display, for what it is or appears to be. He is vigilant. He is wary. He is awaiting a sign, a resolutory clue that will clarify to him what has happened and is happening.

Until three days ago, Avvocato Maggioni had none of these problems. His life, if they had made it parade around the Piazza del Campo, would have formed an irredeemably drab, grey procession. Let's see: years of study, a few girls, a wife (pretty but nothing sensational), two children (at a summer camp somewhere), a surprise-free career in the legal office of an insurance company. Add to this: an affair with a female colleague that finished after six months, an apartment in the mountains, stamp collecting as a hobby, a few all-inclusive holidays (New York, California, Egypt), a few culinary experiments for friends on a Sunday. Not much to wave a flag about.

But he had always been happy with things this way, he had never asked for anything more, he had never regretted not being, for example, a famous criminal defence lawyer, or a great financier, a great artist, he had never envied the figures from the world of sport, politics or show business who filled the pages of the weekly magazines bought religiously by his wife. With whom he had always had an uncomplicated relationship, the usual disagreements and misunderstandings to be found in any conversation manual (from "What I really can't bear is moaning" to "The truth is you're just dead selfish, like all men"); and as for carnal impulses, for some reason they had always been squeezed in between remarks of the type "For God's sake let's keep the noise down, Signora Zoli's back", and "Now, if you shift your elbow I'll phone that wretched plumber".

His had been a moderate or even a mediocre life. Obviously this is how he judges it now, looking at it, so to speak, from the window; but essentially he had been aware of this even before and without being too worried about it. He would read statistics on the flu, on smoking, on consumption of poultry and eggs, and would happily recognize himself in the various percentages: that's me in these forty per cent that put very little sugar in their coffee, in these fifty-nine per cent who go on holiday in August.

Three days ago (13 August inst.), in a midsize car purchased by eighteen per cent of Italian car owners, Signor and Signora Maggioni were on their way from Milan to a farm between Arezzo and Siena where Valeria's brother had retired a few years ago to live "a different life" with a group of friends: all ex-managers, ex-bankers, ex-advertisers, ex-something or other who had had enough of the polluted and chaotic metropolis and who now cultivated first fruits and olives and sold preserves and wine at very dear prices; very dear people whom the lawyer could not take seriously.

"But I admire them," said Valeria as they turned off the main road, "they've had the courage to make a clean break. And it's also good business."

"Maybe, but it still seems like a kind of game to me."

"How can you call it a game when their hands are rough with calluses?"

"I don't know, all that stuff about going back to nature, the fruits of the earth, et cetera et cetera, it's just never convinced me."

"No, but you were so sure they'd all come crawling back home after six months with bad backs, and so now it bothers you that they've made a go of it. Even financially."

"I'd like to see their balance sheets. I'd be surprised if they break even."

"So what? At least they're leading a life that's healthier, more… authentic."

The other times they had been there, after a week of authentic life on the farm Valeria had always begun to assume the wistful expression of one secretly dreaming of the shop windows in Corso Vittorio Emanuele on a November evening. But that didn't stop her energetically defending the "clean break" of Paolino & Company, their exemplary devotion to tomatoes, rabbits and flies.

"A more genuine life," she reaffirmed.

Between short resumptions of the discussion and prolonged silences (there is no conversation manual for married couples in a car) the lawyer drove on towards the farm known as Le Rombaie at a moderate speed and with no forebodings of any sort.

Valeria later made the point that he could have driven faster, the road was good, there wasn't too much traffic. Yes, but then: who had delayed their departure from Milan with her final preparations ("Do you want the blue pullover?", "Where on earth is the Portuguese shawl?") And in addition: if there hadn't been such a long queue at the Melegnano tollbooth… if they hadn't stopped for lunch in Parma… if…

The truth, thinks Maggioni, is that his wife, like all women, finds it hard to accept the idea of destiny – or of chance, to use a less grim word. She needs to trace the chain of events back link by link to discover the one she feels is crucial, decisive: the culprit to be seized by the neck. Even if nothing can be done about it now, she is left with the consolation (a meagre, pointless one) of thinking that one might have intervened, acted, sidestepped or taken preventive action. And she finds nothing illogical in including among the culprits the date of the thirteenth, notoriously inauspicious for travellers.

Any "reconstruction of events", even over a broken cup, should retrace the entire labyrinth of the past, examining every turning, every crossroads, every fork; it should recalculate from top to bottom the inconceivable sum of all data, both large and small, that lead all the way back to Adam and Eve.

But to be practical, reflects the lawyer, the most reasonable starting point in our case is the hailstorm. It's true: an hour earlier, an hour later, they would have avoided it. Let's say that destiny (*la sorte*, they call it in Siena) decided otherwise, and let us reconstruct the encounter between this average couple, a little tired and sleepy from their journey, with a gathering of storm clouds that had amassed on 13 August, towards evening, over the hills between Arezzo and Siena.

II

Gazing at the historical procession as it parades through the Piazza del Campo, and considering its solemn but also meticulous progress, where every movement, every gesture, is part of a ceremonial elaborated over centuries, the very last thing one would think of is chance. In all this pomp there is nothing that is not studied, calculated, channelled and regulated; and the city itself, compact and rigid in its medieval severity, seems to exclude the whims and caprices of haphazardness. The only thing entrusted to *la sorte*, in the Palio, would appear to be the race itself.

But that is not actually the case. *La sorte* rules the Palio; it is one of its codified protagonists, long before the actual race begins. The crimson drummer of the Tower, who is pounding away beneath the window where Avvocato Maggioni stands, and the standard-bearers of the She-wolf, who are pirouetting with their black-and-white silks fifty yards further ahead, are parading in this order as a result of a *sorteggio*, a drawing of lots, while another *sorteggio* will decide the order in which the horses will be summoned to the starting line.

And the *bàrbero* of the Giraffe, which, barely restrained by its *barbaresco*, is chafing under Valeria's balcony, does not belong to the *contrada*, has not been chosen or bought by the Captain and by the Prior of the Giraffe. No horse belongs to its *contrada*. Before every Palio, a specially designated committee examines twenty or so cross-breeds, chooses ten of them, and assigns them by *sorteggio* to the *contrade* that are going to race. This prevents the richest *contrade* from always being able to get hold of the best horses (but the same *contrada* can, of course, by the whims of *la sorte*, end up getting the same worn-out nag three times in a row).

Valeria, a white dot on the balcony over there, can't get her head around the labyrinth of probabilities that radiate from the Palio. Yesterday (no, the day before), while Guidobaldo was expatiating mellifluously on these mechanisms, she made a great show of taking everything in: pursed lips, vigorous nodding, an appropriate flow of *ah, of course, just imagine, well there you go, I see!* But she wasn't absorbing a single thing; the lawyer knows her well. And he now recalls that it was he, with his remarks, who had obtained some useful clarifications.

*

For a conversation manual on the Palio:

Guidobaldo – There are seventeen *contrade* in Siena, but only ten race in the Palio.

Valeria – Really? And why's that?

G.baldo – The track around the piazza is narrow, irregular, full of ups and downs and impossible curves (a long note on the lethal curve of San Martino). Imagine what would happen with seventeen horses all setting off together at a gallop? They wouldn't stay upright for twenty yards.

Val. (covering her eyes) – Poor things!

G.baldo – And so at every Palio only ten *contrade* race, while the remaining seven get the right to run in the Palio the following year, and so on.

Avvocato – And the three that make up the ten?

G.baldo – They're chosen by lot from among the ten that ran the previous year.

Avv. (after a rapid calculation) – So that means three *contrade* could end up racing in the Palio regularly every year, while four of them could miss their turn two years out of three.

G.baldo – Of course, but what's the alternative? It's *la sorte.*

Val. – Incredible.

G.baldo – And that's not all. Just think, my dear, that this whole game of probabilities is complicated, enriched and multiplied by the fact that the Palio is run twice a year, on 2 July and 16 August, but these two dates, so close together, are not considered consecutive or comparable.

Val. – Oh!

G.baldo – July goes with July, August with August, as they say here. The two chronological series are in fact totally distinct, even psychologically. Those who saw their *contrada* lose by a whisker (of *la sorte*) in the Palio on 2 July will hope to get their revenge not in a few weeks' time (if *la sorte* has decided that their *contrada* will run on 16 August as well), but in July the following year or two years later, depending on the luck of future *sorteggi*.

Avv. – Double-entry bookkeeping, in short.

G.baldo – And a double passion. All the anxieties, hopes, incitements and rages are exactly the same in each of the two Palios, and yet completely separate and different. Is that clear?

Val. (rapturously joining her hands) – Perfectly clear! It's wonderful!

This, therefore, is *la sorte*, in Siena. Less venerable than Fate, less frightening than Destiny, more elegant than chance, more serious than luck, *la sorte* has here found a familiar dimension; everyone refers to it with affection- ate resignation, talks about it like some weird relative you have to take into your home. It's the eighteenth *contrada*, the eleventh horse that darts forth invisibly from the starting line.

*

All the colours had drained away from the countryside, but the lawyer had not noticed; he vaguely thought that twilight had arrived. There were no other forewarnings. The change came about brusquely and thunderously, as if the car had ripped through a curtain stretched across the road. The dry, grey asphalt abruptly came to an end and the wheels veered across an already thick layer of glutinous pellets.

Swearing under his breath (but, retrospectively, he now sees the trusty X-100 tyres that absorb the skid), he decelerated cautiously and straightened the car, while in the dark his hand searched for the wiper switch. Valeria, who was dozing by his side, sat up and peered beyond the waving wipers.

"What's happening?"

"Hail."

They were blinded by a flash of lightning that sketched an immense torn spider's web across the clouds. In the rolling crash of thunder that followed, Valeria's voice could be heard as if calling from a distant hill: "Stop, stop!"

The lawyer turned on the headlights and indicated as he steered to the right. The car slowly left the road and ran aground alongside a ditch, over a thin rectangle of yellow slime.

"Where are we?"

"About twelve miles from Siena."

"What a nuisance, we were almost there."

The steady, aggressive thrumming of the hail sounded like the reaction of angered insects, of millions of furiously champing jaws. It was impossible to see beyond arm's length except in the spasmodic lightning flashes. The pellets bounced high and thick on the bodywork, on the windows, on the roof, and along with the hostile rattling they spread an icy cold through the bruised interior of the car. The couple both sat there for a long time in silence, in the stunned intimacy of castaways, stranded in an unknown land, isolated and powerless.

Then a lightning bolt struck close by with a heavy wooden crash, as if the scaffolding of heaven had collapsed.

For a conversation manual during a summer storm:

"I'm scared. I always feel it's got it in for me."

"The lightning? Don't flatter yourself."

"And what if it strikes the car? Metal attracts it, doesn't it?"

"The tyres isolate us."

"Look at the ditch, it's overflowing, I hope there's not going to be a flood."

"Don't talk nonsense. Come on, let's smoke a cigarette."

"I don't feel like it. I'm scared. And it's cold too."

"Shall I turn on the heating?"

"In mid August! And to think that it was thirty-six degrees in Milan."

Outside, the darkness was lifting imperceptibly and a vague world was beginning to resume shape and colour around the car. Through the dwindling threads of hail they began to make out a heap of gravel, a twisted tin can, a gorse bush. From the west came a tremendous gust of wind, leaving behind the tattered shreds of a field with blackened stubble, a shaken walnut tree. On the road, a few yards away, rumbled the tall and hazy parallelepiped of an articulated truck.

"If those things can move then so can we. I don't like being stuck here."

"It's dangerous, visibility is reduced by seventy-five per cent."

"Oh, come on, it's more dangerous here, with this ditch that could sweep us away at any moment."

In this reconstruction, the lawyer reflects, what clearly emerges is the husband's submission (or cowardice). He could have held out, insisted on caution, prudence. Instead, even though he wasn't remotely affected by his wife's apprehensions, he had agreed to set off again.

And it had been like driving through a fuzz of television static, like forcing his way (he remembers now that this is exactly what he had thought) through a whirl of electronic minutiae.

III

There are seventeen *contrade* in Siena, and even for a Sienese it's not that easy to remember them all straight off. Anyone can reel off six or seven: Goose, Wave, Caterpillar, Giraffe, She-wolf, Porcupine, Seashell. But then people begin to stumble: Unicorn... Eagle... Panther... Giraffe... no, I've already said Giraffe... Ram ... Dragon, Owl... Caterpillar?... Oh yes, already counted Caterpillar... ah, Tortoise, Porcupine...

And the Forest, of course, which is arriving right now below the window.

The beautiful fawn (or gazelle) beside the lawyer has her left wrist in plaster (a riding accident) and doesn't applaud the standard-bearers from her *contrada*, which is, of course, the Forest. But she slips from her neck the green and orange scarf with the symbol of the rhinoceros, and waves it with moderation.

Ginevra is twenty and lives in Florence, where it appears she is studying something or other. But she was born here, in the *contrada* of the Forest, and when she came into the world she was ceremoniously presented with this silk scarf, an eternal pledge of belonging and of fealty to the *contrada*.

"But let's suppose by some accident of *la sorte* you were born outside Siena, for whatever reason. What happens in these cases?"

"I don't know."

"Or you were born in a taxi while your mother was on the way to the clinic. Is it the *contrada* of the mother, the father, the one the taxi is passing through, or perhaps the *contrada* of the taxi driver that counts?"

"I don't know."

"And what happens with those *contrade* where the clinics and maternity hospitals are situated? They should have more *contradaioli* than all the others, shouldn't they? In fact, in the end they should be the only ones left."

"I don't know, I can't remember, you should ask Guidobaldo or my grandmother, who was Captain of the Seashell. They're the ones who know all these fiddly details. I'm sorry to say I've lost interest, to tell the truth."

But it's not true, thinks the lawyer. Ginevra, too, has heard them talking about the Palio for years and years; from her childhood she has absorbed the passion and the fiddly details. And so there are two possibilities:

either she's displaying the indifference typical of her age for "outdated" things and polemically rejecting the obligation to "always bear the *contrada* in your heart", as the city's rhetoric would have it; or she's pretending to be detached in order to conceal an attachment that is actually excessive, morbid, desperate and dangerous.

Is she a dangerous girl, this little kitten who could be compared to a madonna, a fairy, an angel? Avvocato Maggioni has been asking himself this for two days. He wonders whether he will end up trampled or impaled by the rhinoceros. And, in the meantime, among all these symbols, he too is beginning to see things from a heraldic point of view. What animal would suit his banner? A fly in a cobweb? A fish on a hook? A moth by a flame? That girl is leading you by the nose, Valeria had said just this morning as she perfumed herself (excessively) for her Guidobaldo. As if she too, in her turn...

The lawyer gazes pityingly at the white dot that is Valeria on the distant balcony with its red drapes; he imagines her lips silently stumbling over the list of the *contrade*, which she would love to be able to rattle off like a machine gun.

"Forest She-wolf Tower Seashell Giraffe Tortoise... Dragon... Eagle... Tower... No, I've already said Tower."

"Watch out!"
    "I saw it!"

The great mass of the truck, now travelling very slowly, was swaying in front of them, the position lights a moribund pink; on both sides, the double wheels, like those of a gigantic scythe-bearing chariot, were armed with menacing blades of water.

The lawyer followed at a safe distance; he had no intention of attempting to overtake in these conditions. To their right, ruddy dark-brown hills struggled to emerge from the blankness, revealing now a smear, now a generic fragment of an olive grove, now five or six crows rooted to the ground, glistening, impassive fowls of the flood.

The parapet of a bridge was silhouetted, then disappeared in the tempest.

"Hey! Isn't that it?" shouted Valeria, jerking round.

Before arriving at the farm there was indeed a bridge; but it came after a low hump, and the lawyer hadn't seen any humps (for him, let it be said parenthetically, these primitive reference points – the little bridge, the sunflower field on the right, the old well on the left et cetera, of which Paolino & Co. are so proud and which are part of their "clean break" with civilization – merely cause confusion).

Conversation on the clean break:

"I don't get why they don't put up a sign, or at least an arrow. How are people supposed to know that they sell olive oil and all those other things?"

"They're not interested in drive-by customers any more, quite the contrary. They only work for connoisseurs, for a select few, they've got a whole sales network that —"

"… that makes Fiat and IBM green with envy."

"You can say that again. They've got people who come from Zurich, from Frankfurt, to get their oil and their onions and their jams —"

"In my opinion, people who buy jam at three times the normal price —"

"But theirs is special, made with a recipe from 1912, which Graziella's grandmother —"

In a reconstruction every detail, however small, may be important. And so mention should be made of a soaked shape that appeared incomprehensibly at this point from the direction of Siena and which, for a few seconds, could be seen as a huge motorbike loaded with bags and cases, the cyclist black with water and rubber, his girlfriend clinging to him desperately.

The lawyer would never see them again, but he was distracted by thoughts along the lines of: crazy, on just two wheels, what on earth makes them do it, et cetera. Valeria interrupted him with a shriek: she had spotted the low wall of a bridge and beyond it a tree-lined avenue that set off at an angle from the road and disappeared upwards.

"That's it! We're here!"

"But the hump."

"You weren't paying attention! I tell you this is the driveway! Turn off! Turn off!"

She couldn't wait to snuggle down among the jams and flies from 1912, to sit down by a blazing fire clutching a grappa costing sixty francs, fifty-five deutschmarks, thirty dollars a bottle.

That, in the course of events as modified by the storm, was the crucial instant. The hail had mostly stopped, although it had been replaced by an equally vehement downpour of rain that blurred details, as in a print taken from a worn-out matrix. Nonetheless, since his wife was so positive and pressing, since he himself wanted to get out of this downpour once and for all, and lastly, since *la sorte* is *la sorte*, Avvocato Maggioni, after a brief hesitation, steered through the two plain brick pillars. There was no gate.

The sky continues to be an incredible blue.

The bell of the Torre del Mangia continues its solemn tolling.

The band beneath the Palazzo Comunale continues its silvery fanfare.

From Via del Casato, a black gash in the clay flanks of the palaces, the historic procession continues, *contrada* after *contrada*.

31

Eight *contrade* have entered the piazza so far, the lawyer diligently counts: the first (which has now reached the curve of San Martino) is the Wave, followed by the Giraffe; then the Eagle, then the Porcupine, then the She-wolf (which is now performing beneath the Circolo degli Uniti), then the Tower, then the Forest (still beneath his window, which is positioned twenty yards before the starting line, which is also known as "the ropes", also known as "*la mossa*", the move), while from the right the Seashell is approaching. Eight. Two more, and the ten competitors will all be present. Then the seven who are not racing this year will arrive, followed (as is the tradition) by representatives of the six *contrade* that no longer exist. And finally the Chariot, drawn by four oxen and bearing It: the Palio (also known as the Rag, also known as the Drappellone, the Great Drape), a silk flag hanging from a halberd, which becomes the property of the winning *contrada*.

Endless rules, but also countless exceptions and precedents, as the lawyer has begun to understand. Dr De Luca himself, the Deputy Public Prosecutor who is following the case of the suspicious death up at the villa, told him yesterday evening that he himself, after six years in Siena, still can't make head or tail of the code and terminology of the Palio.

"It's a foreign language, that's what it is. Everything has a different, special name: the big bell of the Tower is called 'Sunto', the trumpets of the municipality are called '*chiarine*', the procession of the *contrade* is called 'passeggiata' and the groups that parade are '*comparse*'; the pageboy who carries the *contrada* flag is called '*figurino*', the racehorse is called '*bàrbero*' and its groom '*barbaresco*'; the parade horse ridden by the jockey is called '*soprallasso*', and every jockey has his own nickname."

The lawyer looks at the impeccable azure glaze above the geometrical line of the roofs and wonders whether the sky, too, has another name in Siena. And maybe he himself does, now that he's here: Avv. Lorenzo (Enzo) Maggioni, also known as...

The road climbed straight and yellow with sludge between the regular double file of trees, stiff cypresses alternating with umbrella pines, whose manes of foliage were dishevelled by the wind. Valeria was looking around herself, already relieved; the lawyer was looking worriedly at the road surface, shockingly riddled with bumps, holes, ridges, two-foot furrows, which forced him into a slippery gymkhana. The incline was at least twelve per cent, and the sludge was descending like a lava slide in which even the trusty X-100 tyres struggled to get a grip.

"Never seen such a terrible road."

"You'd like everything covered in cement and asphalt."

"No, but what would it take to spread a few truck-loads of gravel?"

"Remaking a road like this is extremely expensive."

"But I thought that with all their jams, money was no —"

"What's that got to do with it? They came here for idealistic reasons, not to get rich."

"But you said —"

A glossy black dog came bounding towards them, barking, and Valeria greeted it with pointless affection as it ran alongside the car to make the driving even more difficult.

"Ciao, Bobo, dear Bobo. Do you see? He's recognized me."

The lawyer couldn't recognize the driveway; he swerved and counter-swerved on the increasingly slimy mud, aiming towards a grey membrane glimpsed between two pine trees, two cypresses, two pine trees, two cypresses, and in constant danger of slamming the back or the front of the car into the tree trunks (or the dog). But it must have been his concentration on the driving that made the ascent seem longer than the last time.

Finally, the so-called road curved to the right, lost its trees and became less steep and less slippery (although the surface remained atrocious) as it clambered up the hill in a series of hairpin bends. They reached a kind of rustic belvedere, with battered benches around a battered table; from this rotunda another rutted path descended towards a valley to the side. The lawyer stopped at the fork.

"Up or down?"

"Up, up, the farm is almost at the top."

"I know, but I also remember a stretch of road going down, there was a drystone wall that —"

"Look, look! Horses!"

In the rain they could just make out sleek, slender shapes galloping in a group on the nearby hillside, their heads lowering and then jerking brusquely heavenwards, their tails thrashing in the wind. In a single instant the whole confused pack ran slantwise across a strip of open land and disappeared into the thick scrub, following some invisible path.

"Are they wild horses?"

"I don't think so, they must be Paolino's horses, he mentioned that he wanted to open some stables."

"To rustle up some more spare change? Hurray for idealism."

"Horses are beautiful animals, and everyone rides in Tuscany. It's a very popular sport, and if you live in the country, you might as well —"

"If it turns a profit, all the better for them."

"You really can't think of anything else."

"Sorry, but it's they who can't think of anything else. Onions, jams, horses… What's the betting that in the meantime they've opened a charming restaurant offering local dishes."

"And what would be wrong with that? It's much better than working in Milan, in an office."

Take that, said the lawyer to himself.

And when, after another two or three hundred yards of bone-shaking swerves, they arrived in a vast open space at the top of the hill, he at once took in the paved surface, the balustrade, a row of lemon bushes in earthenware vases, and for a fraction of a second he thought, well, what do you know, forget the restaurant, they've gone straight for Grand Hotel!

Then he looked at the farmhouse, which in the chiaroscuro of the rain had become a villa half-covered in creepers, with mullioned windows, a noble loggia, grey statues, grey coats of arms embedded in the plaster, and he realized they had come to the wrong place.

IV

Around the concave, sloping Piazza del Campo (which is shaped like a shell and paved in herringbone tiles) runs a ring of stone just over three hundred yards in length. On this perimeter, five days before the Palio, a special mixture of tuff and sand, conserved and carefully guarded from year to year in certain cellars of the municipal warehouses, is spread and pressed down to a depth of eight inches and a width of twenty-four and a half feet. They then declare that "the earth is in the piazza", which means that race fever has now reached an acute phase.

The race (also known as the "*carriera*", or "spurt") is very short. The horses, ridden bareback by the jockeys, have to run three times round the piazza, and they do it in about a hundred seconds. But that minute and a half, long awaited, prepared, imagined and dreamed of for the whole year by the whole city, and intolerably repressed by the deliberately tormenting dilation of the historic procession, finally explodes with a liberating frenzy that has no equal in any other competition in the world. It's like the sudden release of an immense spring, like a volcanic eruption, like a dam burst, like —

Val. (with supreme casualness) – Like an orgasm.

G.baldo – That's it, exactly.

Avv. (to himself) – Oh, for heaven's sake.

G.baldo – If you forget this, you understand nothing about the Palio. The climax is lightning-swift, but the tension has been building up, swelling, for the whole year.

Val. (intelligent tone) – An erection that lasts 365 days, in short.

G.baldo (same tone) – That's a comparison I've often thought of myself.

Avv. (to himself) – Filthy pigs.

The lawyer remembers that it wasn't the filthy pig, however, who opened the car door for Valeria, inviting her to step out under his large green umbrella, but a young Filipino – or anyway Asian – servant, almond eyes, dark skin and full head of jet-black hair. The downpour made explanations difficult, with Valeria saying "you tell him" over and over, himself leaning out to shout that they'd made a mistake, and the servant standing there silently and smiling enigmatically.

(What language do Filipino people speak? he remembers wondering. Spanish? English? Filipino? Apart from the fact, given that he knew nothing about it, the servant might not be Filipino at all.)

Then from the loggia there emerged the tall, aristocratic figure of not-yet Guidobaldo, who, ignoring the weather, walked at a normal pace straight up to the car and cut short the couple's squabble ("I realized something was wrong too, Paolino's avenue is all cypresses." "But you even recognized the dog!"), inviting them authoritatively to come in out of the downpour, take shelter in the house and phone their friends, and other hospitable amiabilities.

Can the lawyer, with hindsight, now say that he at once thought of it as the amiability of a spider? No, he can't honestly say that. With all his "You poor things!", "But what a nuisance!", "How awful", the man made him feel like an interesting survivor, one of the 0.5 per cent who got away at the right time from Pompeii. He offered his hand to Valeria and with the servant's umbrella escorted her to the loggia, and then came back to rescue the lawyer as well.

In this case, too, it was a rapid but entirely natural leap, and just as he had plunged into the hailstorm without realizing it, so the lawyer now found himself in that vast dark entrance hall, where a pair of opaque globes, with painted coats of arms above them, cast the bare minimum of light on arches, columns, low vaults, black furniture, large portraits of ladies and gentlemen, and on poor Valeria, standing at the bottom of a great flight of stairs that descended directly from the sidereal void. But *la sorte* left them not a single moment to hesitate or to suspect anything in even the vaguest of modes (and, anyway, what other mode could there have been?).

The dog they had seen earlier snarled from its corner and came over to sniff them, while a door creaked open to reveal a tall, bony woman, holding a glass.

"It wasn't them," the man said to her.

Hearing a car arrive in the forecourt, he explained to the Maggionis, they had thought it was friends they were expecting from Rome. Valeria apologized for their mistake, for the trouble they'd caused, clipped introductions were made (the lawyer didn't catch their names, of course, nor how they were related), along with fresh apologies, protestations, commiserations, new "don't worry about it"s and "no trouble"s, and in the same swift, fluid and wholly unalarming way, an attempt was made to phone Paolino & Co. from a recess behind a pillar, the receiver transmitting only silence, giving rise to the hypothesis that the storm had brought down the line as often happened in that area (clean break, lads), followed by an invitation to wait a while, to stay there until the situation improved, there was no point venturing into the countryside right now, those roads and lanes were impossible, they would need an SUV, they might end up in a ditch with their homely family car!

You needn't tell us that, thought the lawyer.

Valeria looked sharply at him, but he couldn't tell whether she was suggesting he should accept or refuse their invitation, or perhaps she herself didn't know what to decide (but with women, he thought, it always turns out that they meant the opposite of what you decided; as usual you had misunderstood them). He decided to accept the invitation in any case, both because he was tired and dazed, and because the ceaseless thunder and lightning and rain seemed, from that haven, truly biblical; it was a miracle they had escaped with their lives.

He also accepted (Valeria would never have dared, with her terror of "being a nuisance") the offer of a quick visit to the toilet "to wash their hands", guided by a Filipino woman, as young and tiny as the man, whose wife she might be, who led them down a short brick ramp, through a little glass-walled loggia full of plants, across a small vestibule overlooked by a boar's head, and then, after a few more twists and turns, abandoned them halfway down a long gallery with tall windows, in front of an oak door that might conceal a refectory, a chapel or an armoury.

Valeria went in first and he waited, walking up and down like an idiot in the half-light, amid more ancient portraits and austere furnishings, revealed intermittently by lightning flashes. The impression of having waited there "like an idiot", in the lawyer's memory, translates the *post factum* awareness that all the ingredients required to make his hair stand on end were already present: unknown villa, overgenerous hosts, Oriental servants, even the floor with its great black-and-white chess squares, on which the sound of his pawn-like pacing echoed in the moments of silence.

He put his face to one of the windows and saw a landscape decapitated by thick, dark, slow-moving clouds, which, between the lower folds of the scrub-covered hills, trailed tattered off-white ribbons. And suddenly, in a clearing of the valley floor, there reappeared the pack of galloping horses, compact but unstable, a swirling turmoil of black, grey and brown backs, ceaselessly interweaving and pushing past one another. It was impossible to count them (a dozen? half a dozen?) and, as they disappeared amid stumpy olive trees and cork oaks, he thought, I know nothing about horses, but if they belong to that heads-in-the-clouds crew over the hill they'd be better off in a stable, it seems to me. He tried to get his bearings; he would have liked to spot and identify Le Rombaie among those hills, but the low sky cancelled the cardinal points, and there was no lone sequoia, abandoned mine, skull-shaped rock or any of the other reference points typical of the Tuscan Wild West.

Valeria joined him at the window and then he went into the bathroom, a large pale room so full of doors, cupboards, chairs and wall paintings that he thought at first he must have entered the wrong room. He was washing his hands when he heard a desperate scream. Valeria.

He rushed out without thinking of anything, but (the unconscious computer of conjugal terror was assigning forty per cent probability to a large mouse, twenty per cent to a bat, and the rest divided between a big spider, centipede or twisted ankle) in any case there was no way he could have foreseen what he actually saw: Valeria still standing by the window and a squat black shape writhing behind her, pressing her, crushing her against the sill.

He added his yell to hers, ran to free her from the dog that had attacked her from behind, and he already had his foot raised to kick it when the animal suddenly rose; he glimpsed a dark face, a moustache, a white sneer – and a tiny man, a dwarf, fled laughing down the gallery.

Valeria clutched at him, sobbing like an intriguing survivor of Sodom. Or Gomorrah.

Mortal animosities divide the seventeen *contrade* of Siena. There is hatred between the She-wolf and the Porcupine, the Eagle and the Panther, the Snail and the Tortoise, detestation between the Caterpillar and the Giraffe, the Unicorn and the Owl, the Ram and the Seashell. The Tower, a large *contrada* (there are large and small *contrade*, rich and poor ones), has two ferocious adversaries ranged against it, the Goose and the Wave.

Nobody knows exactly what lies behind these age-old conflicts, even though it can be observed that the *contrade* that are fiercest in reciprocal animosity are generally neighbours. But whether it be a matter of remote questions of interest, of ancient subjugations and prevarications, of territorial disputes, insults, immemorial offences and betrayals, time has forever fixed the map of inter-*contrada* hatred. It's in the name of this feeling that, parallel to the official Palio, there is another underground one, a negative but equally intense version, whose sole aim is to prevent the enemy *contrada* from winning.

When *la sorte* has done its official work and has established who will race and on which horses, a whole other game gets under way, a dizzying interweaving of pacts and counter-pacts, of mediations, active and passive neutralities, favours, loans, acts of sabotage and oaths, all of which have the collective name of "*partiti*", at the centre of which, quite explicitly, lies the only factor capable in some way of contrasting and correcting *la sorte*: bribery. Bribery of those ten mercenaries who for a hundred seconds will gallop frantically over the earth in the piazza: the jockeys.

"Let's get out of here, let's get out of here —"
   "What happened?"
   "Take me away from here, take me away from here —"
   "All right, but who was it, what did he do to you?"
   "I don't want to stay here, I don't want to stay here…"
The dialogue between these two indistinct figures clinging to one another in the gloom of the gallery went no further than this. She continued to tremble and to sniffle, he kept patting her on the back, caressing her neck, hoping this was the right thing to do but wondering whether he should instead be fetching water or smelling salts, calling for help, sweeping her up in his arms (impossible: with his shortness of breath he would collapse after a few feet) and bearing her off to safety in the car, heedless of the storm.

"I was there at the window, gazing out," said Valeria with a sudden return of normality, "and with all the thunder I didn't even hear him coming towards me… He lifted my skirt, he pulled down my —" She started to quiver and shake.

"Good lord, what a fright."

With her right hand she started to massage her buttock.

"But what did he do to you?"

"He bit me."

"Where?"

"Here."

"On your bottom?"

"Yes." To the utter amazement of the lawyer, she burst out laughing. "He was incredibly quick, he must make a practice of it."

"But who was he?"

"How should I know, there were no introductions."

"Not the Filipino servant, this man had a moustache and was much shorter."

"Whoever he was, he completely terrified me. I was just standing there calmly, and then I felt him right up against me."

"Did he hurt you?"

"Well... he got a good taste of me. Wonder if he liked me."

"Valeria!" He pulled her over towards one of the antique high-backed chairs with large studs between the windows, sat down, made her turn round and lifted her crumpled skirt. "Let's have a look at the wound."

"He wasn't a cobra."

Her knickers were still halfway down her thighs and on the right buttock a slight circular mark, like a faded postmark, was still visible. He brushed her skin with his index finger, all around the mark.

"Does it hurt?"

"No."

"Anyway, it might be better to rub some alcohol on it, apply a compress, I don't know."

"Maybe he was a vampire." Valeria turned round and sat on his knees, putting her arms around his neck and whispering into his ear. "Or he was a cannibal who wanted to eat me all up." She bit his ear.

"Valeria!"

"Take me," she gurgled.

He didn't understand, it wasn't something you *could* understand out of the blue like that. "What?"

"Let's make love."

"What do you mean, have you gone mad?"

"Come on, let's do it."

"Here, on a chair?"

"Here, on a chair."

"You're crazy, people could come, anything could —"

She wriggled to complete the removal of her knickers, which dropped to the ground, a white rag on one of the floor's black chess squares, prefiguring in striking fashion (but how could the lawyer have realized this back then?) the black-and-white banner of Siena on the Torre del Mangia.

"Let's do it... Please..."

While his skin tingled all over with a kind of freezing sensation, the only thing he could think was that she wasn't herself.

"You're joking... it's just not... Sorry, we can't possibly... Come on, calm down, you're not yourself!"

"Yes, I'm not myself."

It was a voice he'd never heard before, between moist and sibilant, and meanwhile she squirmed and writhed... lubriciously, there was no other word for it. Deeply upset, poor thing. In a state of shock. And he himself was in a state of shock. Paralysed with amazement. He jerked to his feet, almost making both her and the chair fall. "Let's go and get a compress, come along."

She strode away furiously down the gallery, and when he caught up with her and gave her the undergarment he had picked up, she crumpled it into a ball and stuffed it into his shirt pocket. "There, a present, you can use it for a compress."

"Valeria, get a grip, do you realize —"

"Ha, ha." She started to sing to herself.

A pitiful scene, she marching ahead with her chin raised and he skipping along beside her, pointing out the seriousness of the attack. What would have happened if he hadn't turned up to drive the maniac away? They couldn't stay another minute in a house where they kept a brute, a monster of that sort, running free. And who could it be? A servant? A crazy relative? Or perhaps just a stranger who had slipped into the villa, taking advantage of the storm? He was talking at random, with the idea that the sound of his voice – well balanced, familiar – might help to shake her out of her overexcited state, to regain control of herself.

He had to fall silent when they found themselves back in the small vestibule with the boar's head, beneath which stood the Filipino woman, waiting for them. They went back with her to the vast, deserted entrance hall and its dim globes, and the lawyer was already heading for the front door, having decided to get away from the villa and all its inhabitants without any farewells, when from one of the two branches of the staircase at the far end there appeared the most wonderful creature (Ginevra) he had ever seen in his life – fairy, madonna, angel, deer, gazelle, with long blonde hair and one wrist in plaster. She was turning towards the top of the stairs and saying to someone: "But if it goes on like this it'll be all mud, they won't be able to race."

This was Avv. Lorenzo (Enzo) Maggioni's first encounter with the Palio of Siena.

V

The lawyer embraces Ginevra, the dream creature that at any second (this has been his impression right from the beginning) could vanish, fade into nothing.

What will the American woman be thinking of the two of them? And the other spectators walking around behind them, passing from one window to the next, from one room to the next, of this sumptuous apartment that looks onto the piazza? They all know one another, they are old *habitués*, laughing and gossiping. They probably take them for father and daughter. A caring father who has brought his "*bambina*" to see the Palio. She sprained her wrist falling off her horse, and so he, wishing to console her...

He even said as much to her, he couldn't resist it (there is nothing about her that he can resist):

Avv. – I could be your father.

Ginevra (who, with his help, was taking off her blouse) – Are you kidding me, my father wouldn't think

50

twice about it! He fucks like a hedgehog, he jumps right in wherever he can.

The lawyer tightens his embrace. The breezy and – how can he put it? – unpoetic language that Ginevra deliberately uses disconcerted him at first, but it no longer fools him. It's a mask, an affectation of cynicism, like her pretended indifference to the result of the race. She talks like that to hide her deepest essence, which has nothing to do with the crudities and vulgarities of sex. This is what Valeria has never been able to and never will be able to understand.

Val. – Ha ha, you like young girls, at last you've fallen for one too.

Avv. – If that's how you choose to see it...

Val. – Just try not to make yourself ridiculous. Ha ha.

Pure jealousy, of course. Or rather pure envy, given that she was already cosying up to Guidobaldo. Or the plain and simple fact that a wife, when other women appear, transfers you arbitrarily from the *contrada* of the Caterpillar or the Mollusc to that of the Ram or the Randy Ape, and in her voice you hear the stainless steel of the razor that would sort you out once and for all, you and your filthy tool.

Except that the lawyer must admit that he himself doesn't understand what effect this "young girl" does have on him. A certain percentage of sex (understood in a broad sense, and to be analysed and subdivided in turn) is undoubtedly present. But the other percentages still elude him. Ginevra remains a mystery, perhaps bound up with all the other mysteries of the last few days.

Val. (passing casually to the *contrada* of Simplification) – What mystery? She's just a little whore always ready to spread her legs.

The lawyer moves his hand over the back of the "little whore" as if seeking a definition of her body (slim? sinuous?), and another of those sentences he can't resist saying rises to his lips. *What are you really?* he is about to ask her.

But he feels her body (slender? lissom?) stiffen imperceptibly beneath his hand, while her head jerks towards him.

"Ah, finally," says Ginevra, looking over his shoulder. "I was dying of thirst."

Behind them there is now a waiter in a white jacket with a large tray full of drinks. Everyone clusters around him.

"What about you? Aren't you thirsty?" says Ginevra, moving forwards.

"No," says the lawyer. "I'm not." He stretches out his hand, holds her back. "Don't go."

"Why?"

He feels his throat dry, but not with thirst. "No, nothing, sorry."

She joins the group, a beautiful, excessively blonde girl who, together with other smiling, elegant, refined people of various ages, is quenching her thirst against the background of a chic house, beneath the benevolent gaze of a dignified servant. But he doesn't want to know what they are drinking; he doesn't want to see Ginevra in this corny commercial-clip setting. He is sure she has nothing to with all this; she doesn't belong to the percentages that drink X, eat Y and wash with Z. (But then what does she belong to?)

The lawyer turns his eyes towards the piazza to change programme, but everything is motionless down there. The music has stopped, the flags are not flying, the drums are not rolling, the crowd is not applauding. Is it just by chance that a grey cloud has covered the sun? That all the colours are faded?

There are now seventeen *contrade* in the piazza, from the Wave, which opened the procession, to the Dragon, which is closing it. All of them are now onstage, so to speak: both those about to race and those excluded from the race this time round. But down there, to his right, in the dark Via del Casato, the lawyer glimpses another group of horsemen waiting to enter.

Ah.

He stretches out his hand to the American woman. *Can I*, should he say, or *May I*? He can never remember.

"*Could you please?*" he finally spells out.

She smiles at him and hands him the binoculars.

Ah, it's them.

Six horses with long caparisons covering even their heads. Two slits for the ears, two for the eyes (huge and wicked). They are ridden by six armoured horsemen, with the visors of their helmets lowered. And their helmets are crowned by the six symbols: Viper, Rooster, Oak, Strong-sword, Bear, Lion.

Yes, it's them, thinks Avvocato Maggioni with a smile, proud of his knowledge, proud that he has recognized them: the dead *contrade.*

The invitation to dinner came after another attempt to communicate with Paolino & Co., up at Fort Apache. But the line was still down; the receiver emitted a hostile muteness that seemed personal, like a deliberately turned back. The break was very clean.

But the lawyer remembers that at that point, despite the apparition of the wonderful creature (accompanied by an austere and venerable old man), he would have left. The storm seemed to be dying down and there was no logical reason why their decision should depend on that phone call. Why contact the idealists? To let them know what? That Valeria and he were late? They already knew that, and they would have nothing helpful to say to them: hello, we're all calm and peaceful here among our tomatoes and silkworms, the

Indians have raised the siege, come right round, *over and out.*

All they had to do was get up and go. But Valeria assumed the air of a refugee, put on a whole helpless performance of what should we do what shouldn't we do, which, given the hour and the presence of all the others around the phone, was tantamount to soliciting an invitation to dinner. Which promptly came from: 1) Guidobaldo; 2) the bony woman with her hair in a bun, whose name turned out to be Elisabetta; 3) The austere old man called Ascanio. Ginevra didn't utter a word, showed no interest whatsoever.

Valeria needed no second bidding, and found a way, even as she accepted, to cast a challenging glance at the lawyer. You see how this banal housewife faces danger and the unforeseen? You see how she enjoys herself in an unusual situation? That bite on her bottom had gone to her head.

They all passed through to the library, surrounded by vast acres of parchment, leather and faded gold, thousands of spines pressed together on the long sides of the room and rising to the ceiling, which was frescoed with pallid allegories. One of the room's shorter sides was taken up by an imposing bookcase, with four twisting columns of reddish wood; in the centre of the opposite wall stood an ornate fireplace in marble and grey stone, with a lovely crackling fire.

"Oh, what a lovely fire!" cried Valeria at once. Never short of a brilliant quip, she even capped this one with the following revelation: "I could gaze at a fire for hours."

They all moved towards it. Close by there were already silver trays with wines, aperitifs, ice, crisps, nuts, olives, and a minute later the lawyer found himself with a glass in one hand and a slim wild boar sausage in the other, gazing at the fire from a deep armchair.

The two women of the house were on a sofa, talking together in low voices; Valeria was chatting away garrulously about her brother, the philosophy of the clean break, viticulture, horse riding, boars that had multiplied like rabbits thanks to the anti-hunting laws and were now destroying the onion crop. But although she was addressing the austere old man Ascanio (very thin, with hawklike eyes and long white hair, and dressed in white linen from head to foot), it was all for the sake of G.baldo that she was being so loquacious; and the lawyer, as he realized this, looked more closely at the man who had saved them from the downpour.

He stood there languidly, his elbow resting on the mantelpiece above the fireplace, his eyes gazing at Valeria with some interest. A handsome man, undoubtedly: tall, between thirty and forty, clearly a sportsman, with a superb head reflected in the wall mirror. But his face? The lawyer was reminded of Barravalle, a colleague of his many years earlier. He was from Piedmont and used to say: "Listen to me, Maggioni: when someone's got a face like a *picio*, a dickhead, take it from me, he's a dickhead."

But can the lawyer honestly state that it was Barravalle (I wonder what happened to him, by the way) who aroused the first faint warning signal, the first suspicion – or rather, the first confused idea that there was something to suspect?

No, he can't. The thread of reconstruction is not so simple; other elements have to be considered: their tiredness after the journey, the violent shock of the hailstorm, the fact he had taken the wrong turning, the sense of alienness he felt in that unknown villa, among unknown people. Even Valeria, with her behaviour, disoriented him. The whisky too, probably. And the exaggerated heat of the fireplace (in mid August!).

The combination of all these factors must have acted on him (an average man, unused to sudden changes, easily upset by exceptions) like a kind of drug. Not that they brought about a hallucination; but suddenly, starting from Guidobaldo's face, the whole scene appeared in another light: mannered, fabricated, concocted. Everything was normal enough, in the chain of causes and effects that had brought him to this spot, beside those cheery flaming logs; but his eyes (perhaps a little blurred, dazed) now perceived the final result as in some way frozen, framed and vitreous. And when Elisabetta, the bony woman who seemed to be the hostess, did the perfectly normal thing of approaching him with a bottle in her hand, he thought: My God, the amber liquid, the flickering reflection of the flames, the warm intimate smiles, that splendid girl over there on the divan, that dickhead's face... it's all an advert for a brand of Scotch!

He felt like laughing, and he would probably, and ingenuously, have blurted out his comic impression to the others. But this gaffe was forestalled by the silent ("surreptitious?") arrival of the Filipino servant, who with his smile... ("ambiguous"? "inscrutable"? "enigmatic?") had an equally disconcerting effect on him. Another artificial, contrived scene. A predictable sequence. But of a kind that he couldn't, at that moment, identify.

"Shall we go into dinner?" Elisabetta asked them all, while the servant stepped back and disappeared into a narrow, dark gap between the books.

Of course, the lawyer said to himself, noting that the gap contained a narrow door on which were painted, in *trompe l'oeil*, rows of parchment spines. That was why the servant's arrival had seemed ethereal... But at this point there flashed into his mind the expression "secret passage", and the effect of contrivance, of banal improbability, was unfailingly produced.

Is it possible, he thought, with a mixture of amusement and irritation, gazing at the others who were getting to their feet and the bony hostess who was setting off with Valeria ("I'll show the way") towards the little door, is it possible that in this villa people can only move amid hackneyed effects and obsolete clichés? Even the incident with Valeria being attacked by a sadist, however inexplicable it might be, what else was it but a scene from the corniest of —

"Aren't you coming?"

Ginevra (the dream creature) was there next to him, smiling encouragingly and holding out her hand to him, as to a patient who might not be able to stand up unaided. He apologized and got to his feet, mumbling something about being tired after the journey and perhaps – an awkward smile as she took his empty glass and placed it on a table – a little too much Scotch.

The girl slipped her arm into his and drew him through a billiard room and a lounge into the formal vastness of the dining room, where she set him down, like a puppet released from its strings, on a chair halfway down the long, elaborately laid table. "Oooh," she said with a sigh. "Bravo." She sat down next to him. "Drink a little water."

He drank a little water from the stem glass and looked around. At the head of the table sat Elisabetta, with the austere old man to her left (then Ginevra, then himself). On her right there was an empty place, then Valeria, then Guidobaldo. The lawyer remembered that his hosts were expecting friends from Rome, and he spoke aloud to show that he had recovered from his indisposition.

"And your friends from Rome, they haven't arrived yet?"

"No," said Guidobaldo. "They'll be waiting for the storm to pass, I imagine."

"Of course. With the phone not working…"

"Exactly."

They all seemed embarrassed, hanging on by their teeth to their good manners. Was it because of Valeria, who, as usual, after her bursts of breeziness, had fallen into an awkward silence? Or perhaps, thought the lawyer, he had put his foot in it by referring to the friends from Rome, connected maybe with some serious cause of concern.

"Are you from Siena?" he asked Ginevra.

"Yes, but I live in Florence, I'm only here for the Palio."

"Ah, the Palio."

"Do you know it? Have you ever seen it?"

"I'm afraid not, it must be interesting."

"Very interesting."

Snatches of conversation along these lines bounced wearily around the table, with long pauses. Nothing happened. No one was eating. The servant stood next to the door at the far end, rigid and wooden. What were they waiting for? Who had the place on Elisabetta's right been set for? Not for the friends from Rome, if there were more than one of them. But if there were three of them, then the numbers made sense. Two places had been taken by the Maggionis, the third was the empty one. But it was strange that he hadn't been given that place, thought the lawyer. Or the older man.

Elisabetta lit a cigarette and blew out a long skein of smoke, but then stubbed it out resolutely in a tiny ashtray next to her plate. She turned to the old man. "Right, that's enough."

He replied by lowering his eyelids.

The woman made a sign to the servant, who picked up a dish from a half-moon table set against the wall and came to serve them.

Valeria.

Then Ginevra.

Then Elisabetta.

The distance between one place and the next around the long table seemed to grow in the silence, and the silence did not have that eager, convivial quality as when people are gathered in anticipation of something exquisite; rather, it suggested a cat pacing around a bird in a cage. The lawyer had the precise impression that the hosts were silent because of the presence of the two guests; without them, they would be nattering away about subjects they were keen on – or, he could have sworn, about one single subject (even though he had no idea what it was). This raised the question: why on earth had they asked the lawyer and his wife to stay? What was the real reason for all this fine hospitality?

He met Valeria's eyes but couldn't work out whether she was wondering the same thing.

And in that silence he heard someone in the distance vigorously whistling "La donna è mobile", rapid, crisp footsteps approaching, then a door opening behind him. He was just in time to see Valeria's eyes open wide, and to hear a stridulous voice call out: "*Buon appetito, everyone!*"

He turned around. Tightly swaddled in a miniature double-breasted blazer with silver buttons, a striped tie, close-fitting white trousers and little white shoes with high heels, Valeria's attacker, the maniac, the monster, was taking the empty place between his victim and the hostess. "You did well to begin without me," he said with sarcastic emphasis. "I always like to start at a gallop."

Guidobaldo, who was sitting opposite the lawyer, imperceptibly rolled his eyes heavenwards and turned to Valeria. "Let me introduce Puddu, also known as Ganascino," he said solemnly. "The king of the Palio jockeys."

"But we already know each other," cried Puddu. Baring his teeth in a small, happy sneer, he leaned towards Valeria and delicately bit her earlobe.

VI

The *contrade* of Siena, of which there are now seventeen, were far more numerous in the Middle Ages.

Avvocato Maggioni knows or remembers hardly anything about the Middle Ages, but he has recently been informed (by the erudite old man, Ascanio) that the dominion of the Longobards once extended as far as here. Really? Really. And so the *contrade* of Siena organized themselves around their parish churches, barely tolerated by the barbarian invaders; the *contradaioli* would gather together not only to pray (which they must have needed to do often) but also to discuss their grave plight as victims of conquest, occupation and dominion. Then came the Franks (ah, yes), who installed a different kind of relationship with the Church (yes, of course), recognized the system of local government and even encouraged it, granting it responsibilities, powers, duties and various tasks. The *contrade* provided militias and looked after the sick, cleaned the streets and collected tributes. They were divided into three sectors (the "*terzi*" of Siena) and then, when the city was transformed into a free Commune...

The lawyer, who is from Lombardy and in whose veins there presumably run surviving drops of Longobard and Frankish blood, can see no relation between himself and those distant ages; he does not feel the slightest affinity with the free Communes. Indeed, as an average man, an average Italian, he still feels, as a hangover from his schooldays, a spasm of acute boredom, of desperate rejection, at the thought of the chapter in his school history primer entitled "The Communes". Dense, grey, arid pages: even worse than the chapter entitled "The Arabs".

But over the last three days he has been made to realize that in Siena there is still an unbroken thread connecting those dark centuries to the present day. When *he* looks over his shoulder, he sees his father, he sees his grandfather (crotchety, with a white moustache, struggling to open an umbrella in a cavernous entrance hall), but can go no further back; whereas Ascanio (and also Ginevra, Elisabetta, Guidobaldo and every other Sienese *contradaiolo*) effortlessly sees an endless line of ancestors standing bolt upright like skittles, thirty, fifty individuals – lords, commoners, peasants, soldiers, maybe a few priests or monks, each one, as it were, passing on the baton, as with the biblical generations:

Baccio who begat Bindo, who begat Corso, who begat Duccio…

Ah, tradition! What were Avvocato Maggioni's ancestors getting up to in the Middle Ages, around 1200, say? The lawyer hasn't the faintest idea. Total fog. Whereas Ascanio knows that at that time Baccio, in the company of Bindo, Corso, Duccio, et cetera, on 15 August, the Feast of the Assumption, would have been going to the cathedral to bear his contribution as a *contradaiolo* – that is, a candle. Everything was stipulated and regulated meticulously: the weight, price, calibre and length of the obligatory small candle for every single citizen, of the obligatory huge painted candle for the *contrada*, and of the gigantic mega-candle, 100 pounds in weight, gift of the Commune. A beautiful ceremony, one can imagine. But can one imagine that it ended there? With Baccio, Bindo, et cetera handing over their candles and going straight back home?

Of course not. Even a Lombard lawyer knows that one thing leads to another. People hang about chatting in the cathedral square. They admire the jugglers and the funambulists from out of town. They eat the sweetmeats and drink the wine at the booths set up for the occasion. Until one fine day (the exact year will never be known), someone (not even Ascanio knows his identity) gets the idea of organizing a horse race for the occasion among the *contrade*, which are perhaps already divided by other minor rivalries and by a natural competitive spirit.

That was the origin, according to the well-documented Ascanio, of the Siena Palio, which for centuries was not held in Piazza del Campo but along the dark winding crevice-like streets that slice up the city, through all the chapters of the history primer: the Guelphs and the Ghibellines, the *Signorie* and the Principalities, Charles VIII and Charles V, kings, popes, emperors and republics, wars, invasions, sieges, destructions, massacres, famines, plagues. In the end, after the numerous bereavements that frequently halved the population of Siena, depopulated the palaces and hovels, plunged the workshops into silence and emptied the convents and churches, the numerous *contrade* of the Middle Ages were reduced to the current seventeen.

Avvocato Maggioni cannot tear his eyes (his binoculars) from the six horsemen still standing motionless at the curve of the Casato, from the six dark iron crests crowned by the symbols of the Oak, the Viper, the Bear, the Lion, the Rooster, the Sword. Six symbols representing with mournful obstinacy the *contrade* that have vanished, that have been cancelled and pulverized by the attrition of centuries.

But the lawyer is no longer a tourist or a detached observer; these last three days have steeped him in omens, passions, obsessions, enigmas, subterranean and indecipherable intrigues. Now he, too, can see further; beyond the heraldic helmets of the dead *contrade*, he can see the unbroken line of all those who have suffered garrottings, quarterings, hangings, burnings, plagues, famines, and who have, by municipal compunction, been granted this honorary and vicarious presence in the Campo but have been forbidden any redress. Generation upon generation of horribly mutilated corpses, heaps of skeletons rising to the height of this window and in whose name no cross-breed horse and no jockey, however mercenary and corrupt, will ever race again in the Siena Palio.

How would I react, the lawyer wonders incongruously, if my grandfather or some other direct ancestor had been a *contradaiolo* of the Rooster, of the Bear, or of any of the other *contrade* suppressed in 1675?

Those six *contrade*, Ascanio had explained, were banned for life and deprived of their territories as a result of grave incidents they were said to have caused during the Palio of that year. But actually it had been an act of pure despotism on the part of stronger *contrade* bent on territorial expansion. Rather like the partition of Poland, thinks the lawyer, passing on to another chapter of the history primer. And, initially, at least, it must have been difficult for the ex-supporters of the Oak, of the Rooster et cetera to get excited about the new *contrade* to which they had been forcibly annexed. It must have been difficult to accept, especially for those who, robbed of victory in 1675, had hoped to get their own back by racing with their own colours in 1676 or 1677.

And what about you, he is on the point of asking Ginevra, half-jokingly, half-seriously, as his binoculars pass from one crest to another of the six stationary horsemen, *which contrada did you belong to in 1675?*

But then the macabre troop begins to move forward into the piazza, and the lawyer has a sudden premonition of danger, even of catastrophe. His presence here, close to Ginevra, and Valeria's presence over there next to Guidobaldo, strike him as foreshadowing a tragic outcome for both of them. He points the binoculars (and he almost feels as if he were stretching out his hand across the oceanic crowd) towards the balcony of the Circolo degli Uniti and sees Valeria, who also has her binoculars trained in his direction, as if she were gazing at him as he gazes at her.

Their eyes (or their hearts? their souls?) meet and the lawyer is moved. Perhaps nothing is yet decided, he thinks with a lump in his throat, perhaps everything can yet be saved. The mother of my children. The companion of my life. Why did I let us get separated in this fashion, each of us embroiled in our own absurd story? And what have I done to extricate ourselves?

Nothing. I've played for time. I've opted for wait and see. And now...

In those distant lenses trained on him he feels he can read a silent reproach.

In the distant lenses trained on her Valeria thinks she can read a silent reproach.

Poor Enzo, she thinks. The father of my children. The companion of my life. And here I am frolicking around, airily sparkling. But is it my fault he's having his existential crisis, or whatever it is, just now as we start to lead a slightly different life, seeing people who are a tad more interesting? Is it my fault he's not enjoying himself?

VII

The servant was about to pour a drink for her, and Valeria was about to stop him, when the silent reproach she read in her husband's eyes decided things for her. Ah, so I'm drinking too much? And I'm supposed to hear it from him, who was already drunk before dinner and couldn't even get to his feet? She let her glass be filled and drained it at once. Take a swig of that, moralist!

She was feeling in fine form again, positively sparkling. The silverware, plates and glasses were all sparkling, her delightful table companions' eyes were sparkling, the conversation was sparkling (about the Palio: there are seventeen *contrade* in Siena), and she too was sparkling, why not? But she knew that this fluctuating euphoria was not down to the wine. So what was it down to? To that bite by the jockey Puddu (not the one on the ear, the other one), is what Enzo, king of statistics, would probably (ninety-six per cent) answer. But it had been building up for some time, for a long time now. The bite (that other one) had merely been the occasion, the spark, as it were. A bolder version of the kiss that had awoken Sleeping Beauty.

The new Valeria (still knickerless and not at all embarrassed by the secret, indecent deficiency) excited and frightened Valeria. Leave her alone, she said to herself, let's see how far she'll go. After all, there's also this third Valeria, alert, detached and objective, who is aware of every shade of meaning and is keeping everything under control (or so at least she hopes). "Excuse my ignorance, but why's it called that?" she asks Guidobaldo with lively interest. "What does Palio mean?"

It was Ascanio who answered her authoritatively. "From the Latin *pallium*, 'drape', which then came to mean standard, banner. And in fact the winner receives a prize of a painted banner that —"

"But it must be ancient!"

"No, every time a different artist is appointed to —"

"A different poor wretch," Ginevra corrected him, "dashes off a daub with the Madonna and the symbols of the *contrade* that are racing that year. Sometimes 'traditional', sometimes 'modern', and each time more horrendous than the last."

No one contradicted her. The girl was the only one in the group who was frankly disagreeable. She spoke little, but always in an arrogant tone and with a kind of disgust, as if she were spitting out midges. The two men, on the other hand, were softly, warmly, spontaneously, perfectly gentle. That, after all, was what *gentlemen* meant; the word said it all: men who were gentle above all else. Mind you, the hostess, Elisabetta, was exquisite too (with hands as in an old painting, and an octagonal sapphire in an ancient setting of white gold, which the three Valerias kept glancing at irresistibly).

And Puddu himself, also known as Ganascino (or Small Jaws), who kept touching her legs with his little feet under the table as he drooled shamelessly, was no longer terrifying; indeed, his brazenness, vulgarity and capriciousness amused Valeria. He was more of an outrageous buffoon than an actual sex maniac. The others treated him deferentially, laughing politely at his obscene quips and jokes (he had already told three, two of them "old" ones), but it was clear that they put up with him only for complicated reasons connected with the Palio.

From what she could vaguely gather, he was supposed to ride the horse of the Panther, even though this was not the *contrada* of any of the people present (Guidobaldo and Elisabetta belonged to the Wave, Ascanio to the Goose, the girl to the Forest). So why did they have him here, a flattered and undesired guest? As a favour to the supporters of the Panther? But then, via Enzo's pedantic questions, it emerged that although the horses had already been assigned (this morning, by *sorteggio*) to the various *contrade*, the jockeys could be swapped right up to a few hours before the race. So maybe it was the opposite, and these people wanted to snatch the famous Puddu, "king of the jockeys", away from the Panther. They wanted to persuade him to race for one of their *contrade*, or perhaps for a different one altogether, who could say?

In addition to his (presumed) enormous member, the tiny man made loaded allusions to certain enormous sums of money that the various *contrade* had paid him for his services and for his "tricks"; and these "tricks", Valeria realized, must have been out-and-out betrayals, even though none of those present showed any outrage. On the contrary, it seemed that this was the skill they most admired in the jockey: his ability to switch sides at the last second, to race (and to lose) for one *contrada* while having secretly sold himself to another, to hold the horse back at the beginning or at the end, to use his whip to hinder or frustrate the other jockeys, to offer himself up simultaneously to several *contrade*, to break his word, to prevaricate, to lie. An utter swine.

"Torcicollo," Puddu had started shouting, "is a shit! I'll happily give him ten or fifty yards on just one circuit and on any horse..." His hatred for Torcicollo (Stiff Neck), a rival who sounded like an even bigger swine than he was, had turned him purple (along with the wine). But at the same time he reached out to squeeze Valeria's thigh under the table.

"Puddu, you've got sauce on your chin," the girl sitting opposite told him. "Here."

He seemed unsure whether to feel offended or grateful. "Ah," he merely snorted, wiping his napkin over half his face, then clicked his fingers at the servant and had his glass refilled. The others smiled obligingly.

But he must be a really good jockey, reflected Valeria, for them to spoil him like this. Who could say how far their condescension would stretch in the face of his demands as weird petty king? Would Elisabetta or the girl let their bottoms be bitten (at the very least) by the famous Ganascino? Was it part of the traditional duties to one's own *contrada* to go to bed with the jockey? Or was it perhaps a much-craved honour among the ladies of Siena (all the more so if Puddu's thingy was really…)?

The owner of the presumed thingy had addressed her.

"Sorry, what did you say?"

"I said: do you ride?" he repeated.

"No."

"I'm sorry for your husband," sniggered the little man. "And for you too, as you're still a fine filly." He eyed her up professionally. "Properly mounted, you could run some wild races," Ganascino said.

They all laughed politely and Valeria (scandalized/offended but at the same time superior/affable) asked with sparkling casualness about the Palio horses, ah, weren't they thoroughbreds? No, because on a track like that you needed legs that weren't too delicate or too fragile. And how did they choose them? Well, the breeders, the horse-dealers, took them to the piazza for the *sorteggio*, which had taken place that morning, and there the committee chose ten, ten of more or less equal worth (Enzo: ah, interesting), excluding the ones that were too vigorous or too run-down, as well as the defective ones (Enzo: they have to be insured against falls and accidents, I imagine); and after they'd been shared out they held trial runs on the track, but the first one, due this evening, had already been cancelled because of the storm, and tomorrow, well, maybe the two trials tomorrow wouldn't take place either, it depended on the condition of the ground after all this rain, so that —

Valeria clasped her hands. "Oh, do you know that on our way here we saw some beautiful horses in the rain?"

A lively sparkling of eyes flitted around the table, then they all looked down at their plates while a short and absolute silence closed in on them like the last turn of a screw.

Why? What did I say? thought Valeria (I've drunk too much, Enzo is right).

"Horses?" said Ascanio cautiously. "Where?"

"Nearby, in a little valley," she said, a little intimidated.

"Mounted?"

"No, in fact they seemed... we thought they were wild horses."

"And how many were there?"

"I don't know, a small pack galloping past in the rain. Aren't they yours?"

"No," said Elisabetta. "The villa has stables, but right now they're empty."

"Then they must be my brother's, at the Rombaie," said Valeria, clutching at the familiar eyes of her husband.

Suddenly she felt those delightful hosts to be alien, incomprehensible. They were no longer sparkling, and neither was she. When they returned to the library for coffee (no thanks, I can't sleep if I do) she asked if she could try and phone Paolino again, and the Filipino accompanied her to the telephone in the vestibule and left her there.

She lifted the receiver, listened to nothingness for a few seconds, started dialling the number anyway, and halfway through gave up. The Filipino woman, who was passing by, smiled at her and, without halting, made a gesture with her index and middle finger: the sign of scissors cutting.

*

Am I really in love with him? Valeria asks herself as she observes Guidobaldo's profile beside her, on the balcony of the Circolo degli Uniti, also known as Casino dei Nobili. Would I be ready to do anything for him? To leave my husband and children, to steal, to cut off all my hair, to prostitute myself in the backstreets of, say, Naples or Barcelona?

These envisaged developments set her heart racing, even though she knows she is unlikely to be put to the test. But the questions themselves inebriate her; in all these years of marriage the most she has ever done is ask herself, rarely and blandly, whether she might not have done better to marry Carletto, now a consultant at the hospital in Legnano.

Questions: for the last three days she has done nothing but ask herself a whole series of them. But as for the problems, the big doubts, the crises: she has decided to leave them all to her husband, who right now is perhaps scolding himself for not being there beside her to defend his woman – from her own self above all – and to win her back even as he remains over there at that window, arm in arm with that slutty chit of a girl.

"What's happening? What does it all mean?" he had asked her yesterday evening, all serious, grave and remorseful. But he couldn't even explain whether he was talking about the two of them, about himself with

Ginevra or about her with Guidobaldo, or about something else entirely. He just said that there seemed to be "something false" about the whole thing (but what thing?).

Valeria shrugs retrospectively and gives herself up, abandons herself (no active verb comes to mind) to the multicoloured spectacle that dazzles her from the curved quadrilateral of the piazza. Her eyes allow themselves to be invaded by, to be filled with the colours; they absorb and drink in colours, all desirable, from the most violent to the most delicate, all to be worn and preserved in a fathomless, kaleidoscopic closet. Never – not even when she was taken to the theatre as a child for the first time – has she felt such a magical sense of immersion and oblivion. Valeria no longer exists, her heart has taken on the slow, solemn rhythm of the drums; her blood races, stops, starts racing again, keeping time with the halts and advances of the "*comparse*", and inside her head, as blue and empty as the sky, stream all the banners of the seventeen *contrade*: Giraffe, Goose, Tower, She-wolf, Seashell... Seashell... (Ah, my memory!)

Down there, at the curve of the Casato, iron-clad warriors with lowered visors have appeared, their horses draped funereally. They must be the dead *contrade* Ascanio talked about. Eight.

Or six? Viper, Oak, Owl (Owl?), Bear, Lion, Panther (no, the Panther is alive), Eagle... More or less.

This overwhelming variety, thinks Valeria ecstatically, is an image of life, of how life should be. The sheer joy of passing from one colour to another, the intoxication of letting oneself go from one sensation to another, from one emotion to another. Whereas the trouble with men like Enzo (no one denies his merits, his seriousness and reliability as a husband and father) is that they never let themselves go, they're always watching themselves. No elasticity, zero openness, just distrust and circumspection with regard to everything and everyone; and a morbid (yes, morbid) rejection of the unforeseen, a reluctance to take the slightest step into the unknown. So that when they do get wrenched by circumstances from their cosy little corner, they're at a total loss, they clutch at straws to deny the reality of things, they end up going bonkers, quite frankly.

Valeria eyes Guidobaldo's profile, as charming as ever, and asks herself (questions, questions) … whether men are all like that, whether they all have that sedentary, couch-loving, cowardly streak. Take that great hero of theirs, Ulysses, whom they're always trumpeting as a model of intrepidness: well, when you get down to it, he does everything reluctantly; all he really wants to do is get back home, sit down by the fire and forget all about it. It's women who are active; *la donna è mobile*, Puddu is right, poor harmless Ganascino…

"Here it is!" Guidobaldo announces dramatically. "Here it comes!"

A deafening ovation greets the arrival in the piazza of a carriage pulled by four long-horned white oxen. There is a group of costumed extras sitting on it, and a long pole, from the top of which the Palio (from the Latin *pallium*, or, according to some, *palmarium*) dangles like a hanged man.

VIII

After the invitation to stay for dinner, there came one to spend the night at the villa. The hour was late, the roads impassable and muddy, the travellers exhausted, and there were two beds ready for the friends from Rome (ah, a couple, then) who in the end had not arrived.

The old Valeria would never have accepted. Blushing and stammering, she would have hidden awkwardly behind excuses and pretexts, begging her husband with her eyes to save her from such a trial. But the new Valeria was up for anything: before Enzo could refuse, she confessed that she was very tired and really didn't feel like driving herself, given that her husband had poor night vision, et cetera. But he put up no resistance; he was practically already asleep in his armchair on account of his digestion, the second whisky (in addition to the two before dinner and the wine) and the blazing fire. A little earlier he had also stopped asking pertinent questions about the Palio.

"Thank you so much, very glad to accept," concluded Valeria, pretending to stifle a yawn, which actually did break out under her hand.

While the servant was sent to fetch their luggage from the car, the two men kissed her hand and the king of jockeys gave her a distracted nod (had he already forgotten her bottom?) without even getting to their feet. Then Elisabetta accompanied them upstairs to their bedrooms.

Bedrooms, plural (ah, so not a couple), on different floors, with two different single beds.

"Even better!" Valeria said to herself cheerily. "One sleeps so much better on one's own, after all."

This adventurous, bold mood of hers surprised her a little, but she was getting used to it; it fitted her like a glove.

Explanations were given about bathrooms, staircases, corridors, blankets, and when the suitcases arrived the woman left them.

"They're so nice!" said Valeria in an emphatic whisper while she rummaged for Enzo's sponge bag, which ought to be in the brown backpack. "Lovely people!"

"Do you think so?"

"And so welcoming. I mean, after half an hour or so they could have shown us the door politely. No one was forcing them to —"

"Exactly. What made them do it?"

"What do you mean?"

Enzo, who until then had refused to adopt her conspiratorial tone, now decided to lower his voice too. "I don't know, but there's something that doesn't convince me about all this."

"Well, you could have said so, made up some excuse!"

"It's the whole set-up that doesn't convince me. For example, the fact that the villa is still cut off, that the phone —"

"But they say the line is always coming down!"

"Maybe. And I don't like that jockey at all, and you should know something about that."

Valeria smiled with amusement. Clearly the little man's bite had shocked Enzo far more than it had her. "They don't like him either, you can see that," she explained patiently. "It's clear that they keep him here for some intrigue connected with the Palio. And anyway, he's a bit weird but quite harmless."

"Lock your door, in any case."

"What's got into your head? The haunted villa? The night of terror?"

He looked around without replying, but concluded with a yawn. "And check there isn't some secret little door here too," he said at last.

He picked up his sponge bag (which had ended up for some reason in the big suitcase) and his other things for the night and left her.

But if he's so worried, thought Valeria, he could have stayed here with me, or at least offered to do so, made a gesture. No, she thought, as she began to inspect the room, I'm the one that worries him: he doesn't recognize this new Valeria, who's slipping away from him; she frightens him, and so he's trying to scare me, hoping to find his old Valeria again, awkward, shy, terrified by a little hailstorm. Ha, ha.

The room, although huge and rather cluttered, could not have been more comfortable. There was a fireplace (unlit) here as well, above which hung a large portrait of two little girls in nineteenth-century white lace, and one could tell that every painting, every print, every item of furniture (all genuine), every vase and every knick-knack had its own curious or touching story. The softly screened lights evoked former electricity-free centuries (the superbly adorned bedside table bore a candle, set in a whimsical brass frog), and the very smell of the room suggested a rich heritage of conventions, of ancient, admired luxuries.

Valeria opened the drawers (empty) of a fabulous chest, a sensational corner cupboard of walnut (empty), a marvellous closet whose doors were painted with flowers and fruits (empty), then with a smile she threw open an almost invisible little double door, covered by the same tapestries as the walls. A storage closet, of course, not a secret passage. All the same, having second thoughts, she went and locked the door; that shameless jockey was capable of anything (but suppose, instead, it were the charming Guidobaldo who turned up...).

The window gave onto the hills behind the villa, glimpsed sporadically in the moonlight. The disc, almost full, effortlessly carved a path through flimsy tatters of grey clouds, and damp rustic scents of earth, forest, broom and pine wafted up towards Valeria.

It was the same landscape, the farm of the Rombaie was close, maybe those lights up there on the left; and yet she felt terribly remote, in another country, another world. Why, for example, had her brother never talked to her about the Palio? Was it possible he wasn't interested in it?

Below her she heard a door creaking open, and she leaned out to look. She saw the black dog come bounding out, then pause and wait. It was followed by a female figure, unrecognizable for a few moments (a cloud had veiled the moon) but which turned out to be the maid. She was speaking to the animal in an incomprehensible language (Filipino?) and they set off together towards the corner of the villa and disappeared. Strange people, these servants, she thought. Inscrutable. Like her smile in the vestibule an hour ago: of ironic commiseration, pity, warning, complicity? If there was anyone Enzo should be suspicious of, it was them.

A window on the first floor was closed noisily, perhaps by Enzo himself, and in the ensuing silence Valeria closed her own, quickly visited the bathroom (two doors down) and, on her return, scrupulously turned the key in the lock again and retook possession of the room she already felt was hers.

She would have liked to prolong the moment, to enjoy the harmonious furnishings for a little longer, sit down at the small, elegant desk by the window and write a diary page or a letter ("I have encountered a man of great charm, and I sense that he is not wholly indifferent to me...").

But she had never kept a diary, and the only people she could think of writing to were her mother and her friend Ornella, neither of whom for some reason made her want to put pen to paper.

Well then, she could read for a bit. She slipped voluptuously between the sheets (one small imperfection: they were not of linen and did not smell of lavender but of washing powder, the same brand she used, at a guess), and she reached out to the three books spread over the lower shelf of the bedside table. One was in German, a language she knew as well as she did Filipino, and its back cover bore the unattractive face of the author, a pseudo-beautiful woman with grey eyes. The other two were a pamphlet on plant grafting and a volume entitled *The Religion of the Etruscans*, with depressing black-and-white illustrations and a postcard from Copenhagen inserted halfway through it.

She went over and opened the window again (a prudent chink, no more), breathed in the balmy air deeply and conscientiously (were there mosquitoes?), went back to bed, massaged her buttock for a few seconds and felt nothing, turned off the light, and fell asleep at once.

But in the depths of the night (that was what she could have written to her mother and her friend Ornella), it was through that imprudent chink that the most atrocious sound she had ever heard in her life was to enter.

IX

"Coca-Cola?"

"Oh yes, thanks!"

Valeria drinks the icy dark liquid and Guidobaldo, who is doing the same thing, spills a little on his shirt, jostled by a woman standing nearby. With lightning speed, the woman (all in turquoise) pulls from her bag (turquoise straw) a packet of Kleenex and tries to repair the damage. "How awful, how clumsy of me."

"It's nothing."

"There you are, my dear. That should do it, you're more or less decent now." She stands on tiptoe and, half-closing her turquoise eyelids, kisses him on the cheek as if he were a dribbling child. She's a friend or relative; they all are, more or less, on this noble balcony.

Irritated, nonetheless, by this gesture of familiarity, Valeria would like to respond with an even more intimate gesture, to slip her hand beneath the stained shirt and caress Guidobaldo's chest. But on this illustrious balcony, in front of forty or fifty thousand spectators, this is unthinkable.

But have I ever, she now thinks, felt the impulse to caress my husband's chest?

In all honesty, I can't remember. (But him too, for heaven's sake...)

Valeria feels the countless gestures she has had to repress in these years of marriage flooding through her body. Caresses, endearments, outpourings, spasms and effusions, which have been kept locked up inside her and now stab her like rheumatic pains. To run along the beach with him, hand in hand... Roll over naked in the grass... Dance till dawn in a piazza (San Babila or Cordusio?), drinking champagne...

Others have done and still do such things. But Enzo has always dismissed them as unseemly, ridiculous tomfoolery. And what's the result? Nothing more nor less than the crisis of our marriage. He, of course, doesn't want to hear the word "crisis", he even rejects the definition, considering it more unseemly tomfoolery; like all men from Ulysses on, he is lazy and cowardly, afraid to face reality. That's why he has now started to find everything false and unreal.

"Cigarette?" Guidobaldo says.

"Oh, yes, thanks," replies Valeria with a smile at once luminous and sensual.

*

In the depths of the night (as she could have written to her mother or to her friend Ornella), Valeria sat up with a jerk as if her throat were being cut; and the high-pitched sound, protracted unbearably in the silence, did indeed have something lacerating, perforating about it. A shriek. A desperate howl of death. A scream of agony, there, in the middle of the night.

From the window she could see nothing; the moon was setting and the hills were emerging as slightly darker shapes against the sky, which was once again overcast. A truck engine, reassuring in its own way, throbbed as it lumbered down some distant hill.

What was that? Valeria asked herself, feeling goose pimples even down to the soles of her feet.

A nightbird, no doubt. A bird of prey. Or perhaps a mating call between two deer, two martens. But what did she know of deer or martens? A mouse, more likely. The last squeak of a mouse that had felt a great owl plummet down upon it from the immense black vault, silently, implacably...

She closed the window with a shiver, went over to reassure herself that the door was locked as well (the haunted villa, the night of terror, ha ha) and went back to bed.

But that inhuman shriek or howl had filled her with terror, and thus with adrenaline. She resigned herself to leafing through *The Religion of the Etruscans*, pages and pages on vaticination, on the interpretation of signs of good or ill omens, on certain sacred books known as the Tagetics or Vegonics, on the cult of the dead. It was full of funerary urns with squalid recumbent couples, well beyond any matrimonial crisis. And, among the other symbols, there was even a swastika, or wheel of the sun…

She was awoken by daytime noises, slammed doors, voices and rapid footsteps in the corridor. It was almost seven o'clock. She felt unrested, a little on edge, and she had a slight headache.

But it was going to be a good day, she thought, brightening. The charming Guidobaldo would show her around the villa and the garden, the stables and the greenhouses, then they would make arrangements for the Palio; they would meet up again in Siena.

They met up again at the door to the bathroom, which Valeria was about to enter. He emerged from the staircase, and Ginevra came out from a door onto the landing. Fortunately, they too were in dressing gowns, and looked ruffled and agitated.

"What's up?"

"Nothing, nothing, you had better stay in your room." Strained smile, absent eyes.

"Is someone ill?"

"Yes, that's it, I'll explain later."

They rushed off, and Valeria thought back to the terrible nocturnal shriek (a sign of ill omen?) and the

Etruscan auspices. She could no longer remember the exact way to Enzo's room, but ran up to the floor above, tried a couple of open doors, and at last spotted his sponge bag on a commode, his clothes on a chair, the unmade bed. He wasn't there.

My God, thought Valeria, heart in mouth. And I was the one who insisted on staying, he didn't feel like it, he said this place didn't convince him... I've been so stupid. And even more stupid, she rebelled, to get all upset like this, to feel guilty right away. After all, what could possibly have happened? It'll be the old man, Ascanio, who may have had a heart attack or something.

She walked boldly down to the ground floor without meeting anyone, and from the entrance hall, from room to room, she reconstructed the route from the previous evening to the library.

They were all there. Ascanio was fine and was gazing out of a French window with a toothbrush in his hand; Elisabetta was smoking; Ginevra was sitting cross-legged on the carpet; Enzo, in his new red-and-blue silk dressing gown, was bending over someone who was lying or who had fallen in front of the fireplace, which was still full of grey ash. It was Puddu, dressed in a dark pullover, jeans and boots, clutching a hand to his throat and staring up at the allegories on the ceiling with dilated, unmoving eyes.

X

Emerging from a side street, two white-shirted men holding a stretcher run onto the track, pause when they reach a particularly dense clump of the crowd, set down the stretcher, climb over the barrier, and try in vain to make their way through the forty or fifty thousand erect bodies to reach a recumbent one somewhere in the middle, invisible.

Valeria admires the horsemen of the dead *contrade*, their disdainful impassivity, indifference. Not one of their crests jerks towards the plebs, not one of the six horses swivels or lifts a hoof as dozens of upraised arms pass along a body (it's a woman) over their heads and deposit it at last into the arms of the stretcher-bearers.

"Poor thing, she's probably been standing there in the sun for four or five hours," says someone behind Valeria's back.

"But there's also the fact," says someone else (a woman), "that before the Palio they guzzle down ee-nor-mous meals; they always have the idea that eating and drinking give you strength, don't they? They 'give you a boost'."

"Now that you mention it," says a third, ironic voice, "does anyone happen to have a *digestivo*?"

"Ask Gregorio," says the female voice, "he always goes around with his Diger-Blitz in his pocket."

Valeria smiles, thinking of Enzo and his idea, which has become a fixation over the last few days, that he keeps seeing advertisements everywhere. Diger-Blitz, she repeats to herself. And what's wrong with that?

What was to be the first of a series of interrogations was carried out by Dr Lippi, a young man with a blonde beard who turned up on a motorbike a short while later. However, at the time (a thin, crumpled windcheater with YAMAHA emblazoned on the back gave the doctor the air of a technician dealing with some defective appliance) it didn't strike Valeria as being much of an interrogation.

What time was Puddu found?

Around seven.

By whom?

By the Filipino man, who had gone into the library to clean the fireplace.

Had the body been touched or moved?

No, definitely not.

Had the jockey felt ill the previous evening?

No.

What had he eaten, drunk?

This and that... But Doctor, how did he die, a collapse, a heart attack, or what?

The technician rose to his feet without expressing an opinion, asked where the phone was (to call the nearest branch, to order some spare part?) and Valeria, doing her best not to look at the crumpled puppet on the floor, passed through with the others into a neighbouring salon.

Coffee (watery) for everyone. Comments (dismayed) from everyone. But how awful, what a shock, it's terrifying, it's atrocious, it's crazy, it's un-be-liev-able et cetera. Poor Ganascino, an iron constitution, full of life, so strong, et cetera. And yet his heart. Or an aneurysm. Or some other unsuspected internal catastrophe. Unless he'd been ill for some time and had ignored it through recklessness or machismo. Or he might have wanted to keep the thing secret so as not to find himself out of work (would you engage a jockey who was diabetic or who had a troubled aorta?). In any case his personal doctor (did he have one? who was it?) would clear up everything, his family would... Ah, his family! What did they know about it? Not much, there were brothers, sisters... But did they live in Siena? No, in the countryside, somewhere right out in the scrublands, they all belonged to those Sardinians who had come to Tuscany as shepherds fifteen, twenty years ago and who had gradually bought up a bit of land, a farm... All related to one another, or at least friends. And all assiduously engaged in kidnapping? No, no, let's not overstate things, even if it's true a cousin or an uncle of his had been mixed up in a court case of this kind, involving a murder... In any case they would have to be informed, by phone or a personal visit. What about you, Ascanio? Or you, Elisabetta?

Valeria had instinctively kept close to her husband, feeling excluded from the scene and glad to be so. They had nothing to do with the villa and its inhabitants, with dead jockeys and all the ensuing trouble and bother. Two wayfarers who had turned up here by pure chance. Thanks for the kind hospitality and bye-bye, we'll be off at this point.

There was no longer anything sparkling, charming or delightful to see. How swiftly appearances, so inviting at first, lost their allure! And her Enzo (she gazed at him with respect, with real admiration) knew it all too well; he had seen things clearly right from the previous evening. She gave him a humble, penitent smile. But he remained grim and hard-faced. As inscrutable as a Filipino.

Or furious with her for this tragic and embarrassing development. (But how could I have imagined...?)

Or maybe he was waiting for the right time to say goodbye properly. (Well, at this point, perhaps we had better…)

But this point never arrived while they all continued to light up and stub out cigarettes, to talk about the Magistrate of the *contrade* (not a person, it appeared, but an official institution) which should perhaps be informed; and about the Palio, about the layer of earth in the piazza, about the rehearsals at 2 p.m. today and tomorrow, 15 August; and what Ganascino's death meant for the pacts and secret deals among the various *contrade*; and about Torcicollo, Puddu's great rival, who now…

Yes, Enzo was waiting, but not (Valeria finally understood) for the right time to say goodbye and leave. Something else was holding him back (perhaps the rosy and odious Ginevra, who in the violent light of day showed not the slightest wrinkle but just two eyes childishly puffed with sleep?). No one was sitting, and there was a continuous to- and-froing, as with a revolving door; each of the four would occasionally put their head round the door, presumably to check if the doctor needed anything. But had he returned to the library? Had he finished on the phone?

"At this point," said Valeria, inserting herself into a pause, "if the phone is working…"

Ah yes, that couple from Milan, she read in Elisabetta's mind. The latter turned round and said: "Yes, certainly it's working, we've got a lot of calls to make too."

"Just one minute," Valeria assured her, "and then I guess we should be…"

Valeria's initiative reminded them all of their various tasks (washing, shaving, getting dressed, for a start!) and everyone went quickly into the entrance hall, a little less gloomy by day than by night, with dusty shafts of light cutting obliquely through it, as in a crypt.

"Well," said Valeria, "then we had better —"

No one had heard (at least she hadn't) a car pulling up outside, nor the footsteps crunching on the gravel of the terrace. But maybe Enzo was expecting the two dark shapes behind the glass door of the loggia; perhaps he had foreseen, when they entered, the two carabinieri, fresh-looking in their khaki uniforms with white bandoliers, because he murmured: "Ah, yes, of course."

The still nocturnal group drew together imperceptibly in their pyjamas and dressing gowns, while the older carabiniere, with the rank of marshal, came forward, took off his cap, introduced himself and asked those present not to leave the scene for the moment. Those were his exact words: "the scene".

XI

In what scene will that fine guardian of the law be appearing today? wonders Avvocato Maggioni at his window. Perhaps he is sweating and panting somewhere in the scrubland, looking for Sardinian shepherds who have kidnapped an industrialist. Or he's in his little station in the village, reading a sports paper. Or perhaps they have transferred him here, to the piazza, to help out with crowd control.

All along the ring of the piazza – where the carriage with the Palio (also known as the *carroccio*) continues its slow, majestic progress – numerous carabinieri are posted. But passing his binoculars from one white bandolier to another, the lawyer cannot make out the corpulent figure, the broad, absorbed face of the marshal. An honest, conscientious bureaucrat, concerned above all else not to make a mistake; and yet still capable of agitating Valeria, who had returned to her senses after her aggressive jauntiness of the previous evening, switching immediately to an anxious jitteriness as of a lost soul, what's he going to ask me, what's he not going to ask me, what shall I say, what shan't I say. Completely helpless in the face of Authority. In the face of the icy Inquisitor.

The lawyer caresses Ginevra's shoulder; she is a creature, whatever species she belongs to, of a very different temperament, of quite another level of aplomb. It was – he reflects – the arrival of Authority that opened his eyes (and his heart). The marshal as Cupid.

They were all standing there in the dim entrance hall like statues plonked down there by removal men, and it was she, the fawn or filly (or gazelle?), in modest white pyjamas, who took hold of the situation. She accompanied the carabinieri into the library, asked whether they needed a private room to collect witness statements, chose for this purpose a small salon known as the Sodoma Room, and ordered everyone to go upstairs and get dressed and come back down within a quarter of an hour.

"Knows what she's doing, that girl," said Avvocato Maggioni without reflecting.

Acid grimace from Valeria. "She likes to give herself airs. She reminds me of a traffic officer, with that wrist in plaster."

(Never say another woman is beautiful unless she is spectacularly stupid. Never say she is efficient unless she is irredeemably ugly.)

Shaving and washing, then coming down to collect

Valeria with obedient alacrity, the lawyer realized that he himself was, in part, a victim of such prejudices. The creature had struck him, it is true, as stupendous the previous evening; but she was, after all, merely a creature, remote under the scornful, taciturn, obtuse glass of youth. Luminous certainly, but completely unconnected with what was happening, with the grim atmosphere of the rain, of the house. An added touch, highly decorative and wholly ephemeral, one that could vanish in the night without leaving a trace. A dream creature if ever he had seen one.

But anyway, what was she doing in this villa, with these people? A passing guest or a relative of one of them? And why didn't she have a friend with her, male or female, someone of her own age? Or was *she* in fact the mistress of the house?

Valeria took part in these speculations in a distracted fashion. Not unexpectedly, she wasn't ready yet. She was in the middle of the "what shall I wear what shan't I wear" stage, with the entire contents of her two cases spread out over the bed and the chairs.

Called upon to arbitrate, the lawyer remained strictly neutral between red jeans unsuited to the mournful context, white jeans that were too tight, a blue skirt that was too rumpled, a green skirt that was unfashionable, and clashing combinations of blouses and T-shirts of every colour, pattern and material.

He saw the Filipino woman emerge from the back door with a bowl in one hand and a box of dog food in the other (Puppy Chef) and heard the grateful, greedy munching of the black beast that had darted out from the scrub, which began a few yards away, dense and gleaming in the sun.

"Should I tell him about the scream?" asked Valeria, bending down to pull on the sand-coloured skirt. She had taken off a black bra for the second time, which implied the (perhaps) definitive choice of a light-coloured blouse or T-shirt, with matching white bra.

But Avvocato Maggioni was stirred by the sight, in that unfamiliar room, next to an unmade bed, of a half-naked woman bending over in an intimate, hasty and brusquely exciting pose.

"What's got into you? Have you gone crazy?"

"Come on, Valeria —"

"No way, what are you thinking of?"

"Come on —"

"Let go of me, will you? Do you think this is the time, with the carabinieri waiting for us down there?"

"What do you care about the carabinieri? Come on."

"Don't be such an idiot; if I say no it means no."

"But yesterday you really wanted —"

"Cut it out! For one thing, it's in really bad taste after what happened to that poor wretch."

The woman, escaping from the lawyer's clutches, reacquired the splayed and slightly over-heavy breasts of Valeria, the familiar thighs not unaffected by cellulite.

"Should I mention the scream?"

"What scream?"

As she got dressed and combed her hair with irritated gestures (the damp weather of the previous day having ruined all her hairdresser's work), she told him about the scream.

"I wouldn't mention it, not a good idea," said the lawyer. "It was almost certainly a bird. Or a mouse."

"But Puddu did go out during the night. His boots were all muddy."

"What's that got to do with it? He probably went for a little walk."

"And should I tell him about the bite?"

"No, definitely not. Anything he doesn't ask you about, better keep to yourself."

"And what *will* he ask me?"

"Look, just tell him the truth: that we turned up here by pure chance, that we didn't know the jockey or anyone else, and that we want to get away as soon as possible."

"But it's not as simple as that."

"Valeria, please —"

"All right, all right. God, I'm so jittery."

*

Ginevra, on the other hand, was cold, self-assured and calmly ironic as she waited for them down in the entrance hall. "Ascanio has finished, now it's Guidobaldo's turn," she said. "It's like at the dentist. Come along, I'll take you through to the waiting room."

It was a square room, with angular, exotic furniture in shades of red, and antique portraits on the walls.

"God, I'm nervous," said Valeria. "I'm sweating."

"There's really no need, it's just a formality," said Ginevra encouragingly. "Before they take the body away, they have to get a rough idea of what happened, even though nothing actually did happen, as I've already explained." She walked out briskly in her striped Bermuda shorts, and Avvocato Maggioni imagined her putting them on, bending over like Valeria. And she wasn't even wearing a bra.

Another door opened and in came Guidobaldo.

"You go first," said Valeria urgently.

And, passing into the Sodoma Room, the lawyer heard the charming violinist beginning to apologize to her for the sad event and for the troublesome consequences, and she was already burbling her "no harm done"s and her "please don't mention it"s.

And yet the formalities (predictable and predicted questions and answers, which the laconic marshal didn't even bother to take down) left him with a disagreeable

impression of something half-done, unfinished, uncon-
cluded. He gazed around the walls in search of something that might justify the name of the room, but all
he could see was prints; and there were no frescos on
the ceiling. Maybe it had been sold, the Sodoma painting. Or perhaps it was kept in a safe at the Monte dei
Paschi bank.

"And can we leave now, my wife and I?"

"What? Yes, of course."

"In any case, we'll be staying in the area for a few
days. We're at the Rombaie."

"Ah, the Rombaie. Fine."

"You know it?"

"Yes, a lovely property."

"They've got horses there now, stables."

"Ah."

A sudden irresistible impulse, similar to the one that
a moment earlier had spurred him to throw himself
(lubriciously) onto Valeria, made him pull out a packet
of mint pastilles from his pocket.

"Can I offer you one?"

"Thank you, very kind."

They smiled awkwardly, sucking away.

Then the lawyer passed through into the portrait
room, which he found empty. Valeria and Guidobaldo
had gone off, perhaps to phone the Rombaie.

*

(*Paolino*, in his rough checked shirt – But what's happened?

Valeria – Nothing, we're fine, but there was an accident that —

P. – What accident?

V. – I can't explain, it's a very complicated situation, but in any case we —

P. – When are you coming?

V. – We're packing and in an hour at the most we should be with you. Say hello to everyone.

P. – OK, I'll go and get fresh eggs from the chicken coop.)

XII

In an hour at the most...

But his reluctance to leave the "scene" and move to the Rombaie had not been caused by the prospect of fresh eggs and authentic flies, reflected the lawyer. There was that sense of dissatisfaction, of incompleteness, like the dull, confused memory of something not done, or the foreboding of something that he would end up having to do.

The villa was now permeated by silence, a kind of backstage emptiness. The corridors and passageways remained in a half-light, but the rooms that the lawyer peeked in at to see where the others had all gone had their windows wide open so that the sun brought out the dust and neglect.

He opened a door a few inches and saw the library, saw the doctor and Ginevra sitting silently next to the fireplace. The corpse was still there between them: in exactly the same position as before and yet different, perturbing, as in a cruel slow-motion replay. The muddy heels of the boots were all too visible. The trouser zip was half-lowered. The dark pullover bore a badge with the manufacturer's brand on its shoulder.

Having taken in these details, the lawyer softly closed the door and moved away guiltily.

Why guiltily? he asked himself. He had nothing to do with this story, and in an hour at the most he would be far away. But it was as if he had discovered the two of them in an obscene attitude; or maybe it was the death that struck him as obscene; or maybe, again, he was ashamed of his instinctive reaction to slip away, to escape. Was it here, then, that he should have participated, intervened? But how? And who for, what for?

I'll go and pack, he thought resolutely. But the chink of another half-open door framed Ascanio, perched at an angle on the edge of the billiard table with his chin resting on the cue as he considered the position of the white and red balls scattered over the green baize. Their eyes met, and Ascanio greeted him with a nod.

"Do you want a game?"

"I haven't played for years, thanks."

Ascanio slipped down from the table edge, bent over the green rectangle and briskly struck a ball. Other balls scattered here and there, pok pok pok pok.

"Have you already been to see the marshal?"

"Yes. And now I was thinking that perhaps we'd better —"

"You want to leave?"

"Yes."

(Pok pok pok)

"Off to the Rombaie, is that right?"

"Yes, that's it."

"I can understand that. It's a very, very annoying situation, especially for two people who have nothing at all to do with it, who know nothing and have seen and heard nothing. Even though…"

(Pok pok)

"… even though I'm afraid it won't be over so quickly. It's likely those people will call you back when they get here. Did you leave your address?"

"Which people?"

"You understand this was…"

(Pok pok pok pok)

"… was just a kind of preliminary inspection. Dr Lippi called the coroner and the marshal is expecting his superior, or a magistrate, to come from Siena. And those people will want to look further into it, I imagine. We'll have to go over it all again."

"Further into what?"

(Pok)

"Well…"

(Pok pok pok)

"… there seems to be a feeling that the death wasn't…"

(Pok)

"… might not have been natural, it seems that there are two small lesions on his neck, like two jabs, I don't know…"

(Pok pok pok)

"… perhaps caused simply by an insect or even by his razor, but also perhaps by a syringe. So there will have to be an autopsy, and in the meantime the enquiries —"

"But surely they don't think —"

"Suicide in the first case, even though it doesn't seem likely, but then also murder. And since Puddu was…"

(Pok pok)

"… what he was, a man known for, let's say, rather loose morals, always ready to sell himself to the highest bidder, one who had often been threatened and even beaten up over intrigues connected with the Palio, it can't be ruled out, for example, that he might have gone out last night into the scrubland to meet…"

(Pok)

"… someone from some *contrada* to set up or undo yet another of his 'jokes'. And this someone might have discovered that he had been tricked or bamboozled, and so might have wanted to give him a…"

(Pok pok pok pok pok)

"… a final lesson."

He straightened up with the imperceptible satisfaction of the player used to seeing his actions succeed, laid down his cue and adjusted the silk scarf that he wore around his neck.

"But that's what he —" Avvocato Maggioni almost shouted.

Because in that instant he recalled another detail; in his own personal replay he saw the body of the jockey as it had appeared for the first time that morning at seven, lying in front of the fireplace, the eyes open wide, a hand to the throat... and around the throat a scarf.

"That's what he had —"

"Yes? What?"

He brought to mind a second detail – the real one: a few minutes later, when Valeria had arrived and everyone had gone through into the next room, he had given a last furtive glance at the corpse from the doorway. And the scarf was no longer there. Just as it hadn't been there when he'd looked a few minutes ago.

Having taken up his cue again, Ascanio was now leaning on it like an old warrior on his spear, waiting.

"No, nothing, an idea," stammered the lawyer.

He knew he was blushing, but something told him to keep quiet, to change the subject. "Would you like one?" he said, pulling out the box of lozenges.

"What are they? Ah, Scattomints, thank you."

Sucking away, they talked about the weather. Yesterday's hailstorm had caused great damage to the harvest in the area between Arezzo and Siena, but there had been severe weather in other regions of Italy as well. Today the situation appeared to have stabilized on the Tyrrhenian coast, but the low-pressure zone elsewhere was —

They heard the sound of wheels on gravel and two car doors slamming.

"Are they here already?" said Ascanio.

They went to the window, which was, the lawyer noted, the last but one on the facade. In the forecourt was a large, solemn, dark Opel, from which two men had emerged, dressed in dark blue, holding expensive leather bags. A chauffeur in a blue uniform, a shade less dark, was standing to attention in front of them.

"Excuse me just one moment," murmured Ascanio. And in just one moment he walked out.

The lawyer tried to find his way back upstairs to tell Valeria that there was no point in trying to pack. They would also have to phone Paolino again (but had there even been a first phone call?).

(*Paolino*, sipping a glass of macrobiotic wine – But what kind of complications?

Valeria – I can't explain, it's still all very confused.

P. – So when will you be coming?

V. – I don't know, maybe in the evening, it all depends.

P. – But you're both OK?

V. – Yes, yes, we're fine, we'll tell you all about it when we get there. Ciao.)

He smelled something burning and followed the smell from door to door until he reached a ramp that sloped down to what must have been the basement kitchen. And yes, there was a toaster smoking away on a marble-topped table, in a room that, though large, seemed cramped and shabby.

Through an arched opening in the right-hand wall, half closed off by a threadbare cretonne curtain, there filtered sibilant, exasperated voices, and as the lawyer approached, he caught the two Filipino servants at the peak of a quarrel, the man leaning forward threateningly, his hands by his sides but clenched hard, and the woman, a little shorter than him, holding her ground as she spat out a harsh volley of syllables.

When they saw him they disappeared behind sugary-sweet smiles, and at the same time they caught the smell of burning and rushed, catlike, to deactivate the toaster. "Coffee?" they asked him. "Tea?"

"Tea, please."

"Upstairs?"

Uncertain how well they knew Italian (had they already "been to see" the marshal? And how had they coped with him, or he with them?) or how well he himself knew the villa, the lawyer opted for what seemed then the simplest solution. "Here," he said, tapping his finger on an old, encrusted table that already contained two trays with cups, plates and various bowls.

Silently another tray was set before him with a cup and a little teapot; then the two servants slipped away, each bearing a load, and the lawyer was left to himself.

A strip of oily black three feet in height ran all around the kitchen, including the cupboards, shelves, chairs, tables, and excluding various gleaming appliances in enamel and steel, and some showy boxes of biscuits, cereals and detergents. The smoke from the burnt toast was thinning slowly. Slowly, a double file of ants was ascending and descending near the stone sink. What's needed is an insecticide, the lawyer thought mechanically, looking around for the spray can.

The low ceiling, the silence that seemed deposited there like coffee grounds, the half-light trickling through two grimy high windows like murky oil, all contributed to his sudden mood of defeatism. Just what am I doing here? he asked himself, sinking onto a chair.

XIII

Just what was he doing there?

The idea of Ginevra was the first to pass through his brain, but it was immediately followed by other equally absurd (or equally plausible) "explanations". The Filipinos: he was there to watch over the enigmatic couple, who certainly knew a great deal about Puddu's death. But he was also there to ensure that his own *contrada* would win (the objection "What *contrada*, you don't have a *contrada*" struck him as irrelevant). And he was there to follow Valeria's affair with Guidobaldo, and also to weave his own romance with the dream creature. He was there to discuss severe weather and low-pressure zones with Ascanio, to take part in a round table on conjugal crises, to examine household appliances, to suck and make suck Scattomints...

He found himself on his feet again, holding his tray and heading towards the stairs. The black dog had emerged, yawning, from a corner of the kitchen (it must have been sleeping there the whole time) and it preceded him up the stairs with dignified slowness. Together they paced through the ground floor without meeting anyone, reached the entrance hall and the staircase, turned right, following a route the lawyer knew by now. But the dog, which gave the impression that it wanted and was able to lead him all the way to his bedroom, stopped in front of another door and started to scratch at it lazily.

Another possibly significant development, another episode that might be interesting to pursue. But how could he decide between what deserved his attention, what demanded his participation and what didn't concern him at all? The whole villa seemed full of alternatives, rustling with small, imperceptible solicitations, barely murmured suggestions.

Overcoming his shameful inertia, he slowly turned the handle, and the animal slipped into a room where someone was sobbing desperately.

Yes, Avvocato Maggioni has often been troubled by a sense of inertia, unfamiliarity, hiatus, dead time over the last few days, for all their hectic intensity. And he is still troubled by such sensations. The feverish climate of the Palio, the imminence of the race, do not absorb him as they should. The historic procession itself has occasionally escaped his attention, a segment here and a segment there. Weary pauses. Empty moments undermined by reflections on the weather or by pointlessly persuasive, flattering images of consumer products. The insistent question *Just what am I doing here?* And the recurring impulse to break off, to shut down, to drop everything.

But Avvocato Maggioni, over the last few days, has also begun to distinguish the various threads of the plot – of the plots – in which he is involved. Pink, blue, red, yellow, black threads... Every so often, though, the multicoloured weft is interrupted. Grey surfaces speckled with white sneak in, awakening a clear memory in the lawyer's mind: that of the car's windshield in the sudden hailstorm on the road between Arezzo and Siena. It was then, he reflects, that it all began, and it was then that he should have reacted, should have changed direction, turned round. Now it is too late.

Now all the *contrade*, the living and the dead, have paraded beneath him, and the chariot with the Drappellone is now over there, beneath Valeria's balcony, while the leading *comparse* have already left the ring to go and take their places on a raised tribune reserved for them at the foot of the Palazzo Pubblico.

The lawyer contemplates the trampled earth of the track, the long, confused traces left by the procession, and he is struck by the resemblance of the piazza to... the Shell symbol? Yes, on account of its convexity, as explained in all the guidebooks and leaflets, the Piazza del Campo resembles the valve of a shell. But that roughly trapezoid rectangle, with its rounded corners, also reminds him of the glass windshield that he was thinking of a moment earlier, which in turn makes him think of something that is perhaps important... something decisive... but which once again eludes him.

"How are things?" he asks Ginevra, to distract himself from that dogged rumination.

"Fine."

"Hot?"

"A little."

Others, behind them, are talking of the heat. Of what it was like yesterday in Rome, Edinburgh, Cortina, Milan. Twenty-nine degrees, thirty-four degrees. High pressure, low pressure. And thirst: orangeades aggravate your thirst rather than quench it, while tonic water...

It's no use, thinks the lawyer. Impossible to get away from it. "Shall we go back inside and sit down for a minute?" he asks the girl.

But this, too, is a vain attempt to regain something, a feeble pretext to find himself alone with her again, to feel her close to him not just physically, to recreate the unexpected *click* of that morning's intimacy, the spontaneous shift to the informal "*tu*", the thrilling freshness and ease of each word and gesture.

*

"Is this tea yours? Are you taking it to your wife?"

"No, it's for me."

"Will you let me have it?"

"Of course."

"Let's go to my room."

After the dog had entered, she had emerged from the doorway, scowling furiously.

"What an idiot, what a cretin."

The "idiot" was Elisabetta, who was weeping over the death of Puddu, her lover.

"Good lord," said the lawyer. "Are you serious?"

"Why? Does it surprise you?"

"I don't know. No, come to think of it, no." His readings of news stories and literature somewhere included the cliché: lady of a certain age and sex-crazed jockey.

"You're sure you don't want some of my, sorry, I mean *your* tea?"

"No, no, really. But was she in love with him?"

"Oh, come on now. What is love?"

An apparently banal but truly profound query, put like that. Devastating.

Ginevra's bed was also still unmade, but any temptation that the lawyer might have had, and which, in all honesty, he did not have, was nipped in the bud.

"Come on, help me make the bed. If I wait for that pair to get round to it…"

"The Filipinos? Are they Filipino?"

"I don't know. Somewhere like that, more or less."

"I saw them a while ago in the kitchen, arguing furiously. Are they married?"

"I don't know. Anyway, he's really jealous. The other day I saw him making a terrible scene with her over Puddu."

"Ah, because Puddu, with the Filipino woman as well...?"

"With anyone. That's all he thought about, apart from money and horses. Classic compensation for his height."

"You know it seems that his death... that perhaps his death wasn't... natural?"

"Who told you that? No, sorry, not like that, pull it slightly more towards you."

"Ascanio. He says they suspect suicide."

"A person like Puddu killing himself? What an idea."

"But also murder, over some trouble connected with the Palio."

"More nonsense. At the very worst, the nastier jockeys or the ones that play really dirty might get beaten up."

"So who was waiting for him last night in the scrubland?"

"What do I know, a woman, a jealous husband, or nobody. How should I know? But I think it's all in the mind of that doctor. A good lad but deadly serious, you know, like the ones who advertise toothpaste on television."

The secret inrush of satisfaction that he felt made the lawyer realize that until then he had been jealous of the young doctor. "Anyway, the coroner is here now," he said, "maybe he'll be able to see things more clearly."

"When did he get here?"

"Half an hour ago, him and the magistrate. Didn't you see the dark Opel in the forecourt?"

"Ah, no, that belongs to Ranieri and Salimbeni, our friends who were supposed to arrive last night from Rome, the ones who gave up their rooms for you, so to speak. There, all done." Ginevra gave a few more expert tweaks to the clean white bedspread and pillow and straightened up. "Thanks for helping out a poor invalid, apart from the fact this bed is absurd."

"You're very good. Where did you learn?"

"At college, of course. My parents got divorced and neither of them wanted me around, they had their own affairs to be getting on with."

"Is this your room? Do you always sleep here?"

"Here or some other room, depending on the guests. I've often slept in your bed."

"Do you need it now? Should we clear our rooms?"

"No, we've set up things for Ranieri and Salimbeni in another part of the villa."

"And who does the villa belong to?"

"Too long to explain. There's a whole story of a joint heirship among sons and daughters, cousins, uncles and aunts, nephews and nieces, an endless torment."

Ginevra looked around the room, which, in addition to the huge four-poster bed whose iron angles were softened by a canopy of white fabric, contained a number of items of English "naval" furniture with gleaming edges and handles, and a large cheval glass with a worm-eaten frame.

"Fine, let's go," she concluded, picking up the tray. "I'll take this down. I'll have a lot to do this morning, the dishwasher has gone on the blink... Are you OK, you don't need anything?"

You, thought the lawyer violently. He said: "No thank you."

"So feel free to wander wherever you want, just look in occasionally to see how things are going. I hope everything will be over by lunchtime."

I don't, he thought. He said: "Well, first of all I'll go and find my wife."

"I saw her with Guidobaldo a while ago," she said. "They were kissing down by the lake." She leaned over the tray she was holding out in front of herself and kissed Avvocato Maggioni on the cheek.

*

The lake, thought the lawyer, walking out of the villa in a state of euphoria and alarm. Well, who would have thought it.

The Opel was no longer on the forecourt.

What lake? He crunched his way across the gravel to the balustrade and looked down. He saw an Italian-style garden with a terraced slope and the oval basin of a waterless fountain, circled by naiads and dolphins flaking in the sun. Further down, on the left, were trees and bushes, which grew gradually less neat and less well pruned as they clumped together, merging with the scrubland; through their leaves the road with its hairpin bends could be glimpsed. But no lake.

On the right the ground sloped more gently, with a few humped or level areas left as meadows, some clusters of maples and two or three casual cypresses. From a rotunda that held a grey statue of a goddess and a semicircular stone bench there stretched a tunnel of greenery, long and serpentine, sloping down towards a wooded hollow. It must be down there somewhere, the lake.

What shall I do? Shall I go there? wondered Avvocato Maggioni.

The girl could have been exaggerating or talking metaphorically. By "kissing" she almost certainly meant some kind of schmaltzy behaviour, holding hands, gazing into one another's eyes. But a scene like this was the last thing the lawyer wanted to see; he would almost have preferred to catch Valeria in a frankly pornographic posture, with her sand-coloured skirt lifted and Guidobaldo energetically giving her his all. In any case, he would be left playing the disagreeable role of the nuisance, the cuckolded husband or voyeur.

Forget it, he decided.

But up there in the Sodoma Room the marshal was waiting, and the magistrate, or whoever he was, was about to take over, and Valeria hadn't been interviewed by anyone. Problems might arise; her testimony, however marginal it might be, had to be heard; the inquiry had to proceed according to the rules.

He set off unhurriedly, hoping that the path was taking him in the right direction, and he soon met an old gardener with a hoe on his shoulder who greeted him obsequiously, doffing his straw hat.

"Am I going the right way for the lake?"

"It's down there, behind those trees," said the man, pointing backwards with his thumb.

Shall I ask him if he's seen those two? wondered the lawyer again. Instead, he raised his eyes to the sky and said: "The sun's back out in force again, eh?"

"Ah, but I've finished for the day, I've been up since five," said the other, wiping his brow with his arm. "Now I'm going back home, I'll make myself a nice cup of Nescafé, and then —"

"Bravo," the lawyer said, cutting him short.

This too was a cliché, a gnarled peasant figure apparently about to harangue him on cereals and toast, and maybe also, given his bristly cheeks, on the virtues of some brand of electric razor.

He reached the rotunda with its statue and started down the winding green tunnel, beneath which, amid clusters of flowering wisteria, there lingered a subaqueous light. An ideal, almost obligatory prelude to a discussion on subjects like what is love what isn't love, my life here and my life there.

And indeed, on emerging from this evocative verdure, he beheld the lake a little further on down, with a little stream flowing in on one side and out from the other. And on the grassy bank were the two of them, he sitting with his back propped against the trunk of a willow, she lying with her head on his knees, and a flower, for Christ's sake, a wildflower in her hand.

The lawyer stopped with the icy foreboding of what might happen at any second – and what, inexorably, did happen. He closed his eyes when Valeria languidly raised her arm and with the flower started caressing the dickhead's face.

XIV

Ginevra has returned to the window.

In the bathroom, where he has gone to wash his hands and freshen his face, the lawyer looks at himself in the mirror. He is a little surprised to find himself gazing at – in place of flags, horses, palaces, armourers, crowds, sky – a simple human face, his own. Is that it? he says to himself in puzzlement.

Not that it gives him the impression of a handsome or an ugly face, a likeable or dislikeable one: it's just that he doesn't know how to take it. On his chin and along the jawline he can make out the faint tinge of a five o'clock shadow (he needs another go at it with his electric razor…), and he notices that his Milanese pallor has been slightly affected by the Tuscan sun (he needs some of Valeria's suntan lotion…).

It's the face Valeria recognized with amazement on the lake's shore. The lawyer remembers his wife's agitated expression. But only now, in front of this mirror, does he understand what lay behind that sudden pallor: not guilt, shame, hostility or embarrassment but the consternation of someone awakening to daily life, to humdrum reality, of someone sliding down the rainbow and finding herself in the usual metro station: Palestra, Pagano, Bande Nere...

Seeing this face appear beneath the foliage of the willow, she too must have said to herself: is that it?

In the bathroom of the Circolo degli Uniti, which she has managed to locate all by herself, though not without some misgivings, Valeria checks her make-up, compromised by the heat and her sweat. But it is a strictly technical check-up. The usual anxiety (am I beautiful, pretty, ugly, ordinary, awful, passable?) has evaporated. From that slow walk beyond the mossy statue, beneath the canopy of wisteria, she has drawn the certainty that she is fascinating. She recalls with a smile (which the mirror assures her is enchanting) the perfection of the whole sequence: the glints of gold and emerald amid the violet clusters, the first involuntary (involuntary?) contact between their little fingers, his hand on her bare arm, the same hand on her shoulder and then around her waist, her head resting on his shoulder, his breath through her hair and the inexpressible tremor, the chaste, delicate kiss on her forehead, the kiss (less chaste and less delicate) on her lips.

And the perfumed air, the buzzing insects, the warbling birds, the ogling lake… Yes, perfection. The best. No, I mean it, there were even water lilies.

And she remembers the arrival of a forgotten, cancelled, fossilized, never-had husband, she remembers the stunning apperception at the sight of a missing button ("and I swore I would sew it back on for him before leaving!") on the right-hand pocket of his sports shirt.

All three of them, Valeria reflected later, had preserved an impeccable demeanour. There and then she had felt a little awkward, in the sense that Enzo's appearance had brought to her mind the sentence *And now where am I going to put this one?* Disoriented, more than embarrassed. Like when, at the supermarket checkout, you find yourself holding a packet of fusilli that won't fit into your bag.

Half-rising, with her elbow propped on the grass, she fluttered her eyelashes and asked him: "Were you looking for me?"

"No, that is, I, the marshal…" he stammered, with pathetic maladroitness.

It was with quite a different style, with quite different elegance and casualness that Guidobaldo reacted, glancing at his waterproof Rolex and exclaiming: "Goodness, how time flies!" He sprang upward in one agile movement, stretched out his hand to Valeria and helped her to her feet. "I have to run," he explained to Enzo with a smile full of tact. "We'll meet up later." He kissed her hand, and his lips lingered for that brief span that made all the difference between past and future, between life and death.

Valeria sighed happily and then, affectionately slipping her arm into her husband's, she took him for a stroll around the lake.

"You know there are some extremely old carp in there?"

"You don't say."

He seemed a little mortified, but what else could you expect? She felt that she loved him the same as ever, indeed in a certain sense more than ever, but these were things a man – a husband – was unlikely to understand. Maybe he had forced himself to assume an attitude that was too far above himself; he had been wrong not to slap her and punch Guidobaldo (or at least try to), yelling things like *This woman is mine.* He would have vented his anger, let off some steam.

But now, as the opportunity for a violent and liberating scene had passed, all that was left was the route of frank explanation.

"Listen, between me and Baldo —"

"Can you fish them?"

"What? Oh, the carp. I don't know. Anyway, I wanted to tell you that what's happening with Baldo is —"

"It's true they're full of bones —"

"I just wanted to say, whatever happens, for me you're still —"

"I wonder if this path will take us back —"

He didn't want to talk about it, that was clear. He had chosen a third route: say nothing, ignore it all, pretend nothing had happened.

It wouldn't, she wondered, casting a suspicious glance at him, by any chance be the path of the complacent cuckold?

No, impossible. If anything, he was being the understanding husband who represses his pain with dignity and waits for the crisis to pass, confident that his woman will come back to him despite everything. There was also the possibility that he was being the noble, fair-play husband, determined to respect the rule of "let the best man win". Or might he actually be thinking of a sordid *ménage à trois?*

Immersed in these complex hypotheses, Valeria walked back up the path by his side, paying little attention to certain hypotheses that he was elaborating on Puddu's death.

"And you say the scarf had disappeared?" she said in obliging surprise.

But she didn't know what scarf he was talking about, just as she had not followed what Ascanio had said, nor what the two Filipinos had to do with it. A messy business of no interest.

Her interest was reawakened when she heard him

refer to Elisabetta's weeping. "She was Puddu's lover? Who told you that?"

"Ginevra."

"But she's always been in love with Ascanio!"

"Who, Ginevra?"

"No, Elisabetta. At one point they even ran off together."

"Who told you that?"

"Baldo."

She told him the story: Elisabetta's father was Ascanio's first cousin, and so in a certain sense she was his niece. At the age of twelve she had taken a fancy to him, but he was already married to a widow, Guidobaldo's mother; so Guidobaldo, son of her first husband, was therefore Ascanio's stepson. Elisabetta, out of despair, had then married a very young brother of Guidobaldo's mother, thus becoming her sister-in-law; but the marriage had fallen apart almost immediately, because the husband, Guidobaldo's uncle, had lost his head over a divorced sister of the first husband of his mother, Guidobaldo's mother, that is, and had run off with her. From this union Ginevra had been born, and this meant that Elisabetta was her —

Enzo shook his head. "You've lost me completely," he said bluntly.

"No, listen, it's simple: if Baldo's mother's first husband was the brother-in-law of —"

"I'm just not interested. I couldn't care less."

XV

Valeria didn't grasp her husband's crisis right away. Enzo's surliness, his abruptness, she thought as she made her way back to the villa with him, could be attributed to an understandable surge of jealousy. By rejecting dialogue, he meant to punish her, to exclude her.

But a little later, as they were all eating rice salad on paper plates, this explanation began to seem inadequate. A kind of indoor picnic (with a touch of the funeral wake about it) had been set up in the dining room to feed the heterogeneous cluster of doctors, investigators and other strangers who had come to the villa in connection with the death of Puddu, who had fortunately already been taken away in an ambulance.

Guidobaldo wasn't there; he had had to dash off to Siena on Palio business, Ascanio told her. The Filipino man, Elisabetta and Ginevra walked among the guests, offering them cold meat and omelettes, bottles of water and wine. Enzo stood against the wall, apparently sulky, picking listlessly at his plate.

But Valeria caught him casting an avid and furtive glance towards Ginevra – or at least that's how she interpreted it. Ah, she thought, he's interested in the young girl, that's clear.

Then, two minutes later, he did exactly the same thing with Ascanio, though. Then with Elisabetta. Then with the Filipino. Then again with Ginevra, with the public prosecutor and so on, with everyone there, one after another. A glance, Valeria finally corrected herself, that wasn't furtive or guilty but intense, very swift, and immediately withdrawn, like the quick peck of a bird. It was as if Enzo were keeping an eye on everyone there, as if he were expecting one of them to make… a gesture, a signal?

What the devil had got into him?

Their eyes met and Enzo came slowly towards her, holding his plate. "Those two," he murmured, looking very serious.

"Who?"

"Those friends from Rome, the ones who arrived this morning and who were standing close to you a moment ago."

"Ah, Ranieri and Salimbeni, yes. They live in Rome but they're Sienese too. And so?"

"Did you hear what they were saying, what they were talking about?"

"Politics, I think. A delegation in Brussels, some amendments or something. Ah, and a parliamentary committee. Things like that. Why?"

Enzo nodded without answering.

"You're getting bored, right?" she whispered, misunderstanding him. "The other people's conversation isn't much better, all they can talk about is the weather, the heat, the forest fires… But then, with that poor jockey who has just —"

"The story of the jockey is one of them, but there are other stories," said Enzo, studying his nails. "Like that one you started telling me about the family."

"But you said you weren't the least bit interested?"

"Exactly."

"Well, listen," she said. "I'm going back to my room, I'm going to have a rest, wash my hair —"

Enzo cast that strange glance towards her. "Ah, there you go. With what shampoo?"

"But Enzo… with my usual shampoo, Softy-Softy! I've been using it for two years, you've even used it yourself once or twice."

"Exactly," said Enzo. "Exactly." He sidled off, absorbed, with the air of one going over the bill mentally as he leaves the butcher's shop.

*

He did not lose that expression for the rest of the day.

Valeria tried several times to pull him out of his isolation, to break that wall made of impatience and nonchalance, of watchful silences, of private, secret nods of assent to himself.

She tried to talk to him again about Baldo, but he seemed profoundly indifferent – or utterly distracted.

Was he in crisis because he was beginning to get a direct sense of their own marriage crisis? But he brushed off the subject with irritation.

Maybe he was dejected because of the girl?

"That's not the point," he said, shaking his head. "Ginevra must be some completely different business."

"What business? What do you mean?"

"Humph... I don't know. We'll see."

In the late afternoon they met in the portrait room, which served as antechamber to the Sodoma Room. Valeria was emerging from her interview with the pros-ecutor, and she saw him sitting there on one of those weird, jagged red chairs, gazing at the two largest por-traits on the opposite wall. But as soon as she began to explain who the character on the right was (an ancestor of Ascanio's, but from another branch of the family, who had adopted the orphaned nephew of his...) Enzo cut her short abruptly.

"You know," Valeria said, hoping to interest him, "he was a great hunter, he was the one who brought all this furniture from India, he went hunting for Bengal tigers, and of course in Africa for lions, elephants, et cetera. But his wife, who was apparently beautiful, felt neglected and ended up taking a lover who —"

"Who bumped them both off with a hunting rifle?" said Enzo unironically.

"No, not at all. There was a scandal, but then she —"

Enzo interrupted her, shifting his eyes to the portrait on the right, a woman in a ballgown. "And who's the woman? Some ancestor who died tragically? Does her ghost wander around the villa?"

No, that was Violante of Bavaria, a German princess who had been governess of Siena and promulgated the bill of 1729 that established the definitive boundaries of the seventeen *contrade*, with their respective —

"Ah yes, yes, I get it," he said, miles away again.

Edgy and suspicious. But of what? Did he suspect someone or something with regard to Puddu's death? Was this what was troubling him? She then went on to tell him about her interview with the prosecutor, but once again he interrupted her.

"Did he talk to you about the Neapolitan Camorra?"

"No, why, what's that got do with it? He's lived in Siena for years."

"No, I was just saying, since he's Neapolitan… Did he chat you up?"

"Not that I noticed."

He let fall a long silence, charged with mysterious insinuations.

"Enzo, I don't understand you, what's going on, what's got into your head? You don't want to confide in me, after all I'm —"

He raised his hand. "I know, you're my wife, my life companion, I have to trust you, you have to trust me, we have to trust each other, et cetera, et cetera."

"What do you mean, et cetera?"

"The usual things. The usual phrases. And now of course you're about to burst into tears."

"Enzo, please, don't talk like that."

"Enzo, please, don't talk like that," he repeated, but with a kind of meditative sigh, without imitating her, without the least sarcasm. He resembled someone who was listening hard to check or to recognize a sound. *To verify it.*

Valeria had never heard him sound so distant, so… unreachable, and she really did feel like crying.

At that very second, framed in the window of the Indian Room, there appeared the half-length portrait of Guidobaldo: close, easily reachable. And Valeria immediately forgot all apprehension, uncertainty, mis-understanding. "You're back," she said in a faint voice.

"Yes."

Their gazes merged like two opposing puffs of spray in what was already the dim twilight.

Enzo made another obscure remark about a pink cloud, but Valeria was no longer listening to him.

XVI

A tiny pink cloud is crowning the Torre del Mangia when Valeria returns from the bathroom to the balcony of the Circolo, and all the surfaces of the piazza – walls, textiles, human faces – begin to take on that soft, crepuscular aura.

The uncertainty of the race will now have the added component of a first faint uncertainty of light – that, too, perhaps calculated and foreseen, as poor Enzo will suspect.

Throughout the whole of the previous day, and the whole of today, they have hardly talked to one another. But Valeria has seen him quite clearly, at various moments and in various parts of the villa and the garden, and this morning in various parts of Siena, walking around with that increasingly absorbed and brooding expression, that sidelong gaze hardened by all sorts of calculations and suspicions.

And so all the gentle beauty of this great shell is wasted on him, as he will see it as a cold cavern, a blank screen. And so everything escapes him. And so – thinks Valeria – he is not living.

When he returns to the window, Avvocato Maggioni finds his place occupied. Between Ginevra and the American woman there now stands, in three-quarter profile, a man wearing a tartan jacket and holding a glass.

The question immediately arises: is he somebody or nobody? Or rather: does he have something or nothing to do with it?

And so that niggling worry of two days earlier – when the lawyer first began to ask himself: what do I have to do with it, what am I doing here? – is flipped on its head.

Now it's the others, their presences, actions, gestures and words, that have to fit into some sort of ill-defined scheme (or filing system? or crossword puzzle?) that he has (gradually, unintentionally) elaborated, whose final meaning still escapes him. But he feels he is getting close, very close to the heart of so many, too many, insidious cross-connections.

When he arrives the man in the tartan jacket smiles vaguely and draws back: he's a nobody then, there to fill out the crowd, a tourist extra who has strolled over from some other window of the apartment to have a glance at the Campo from this slightly different angle.

Naturally the lawyer has the feeling he has seen him somewhere before; but it's a feeling he is resigned to by now, one that never abandons him for a single minute and that is aroused by everything that makes an impression on his retina. Besides, it is possible, indeed probable, that the man is someone he has, indeed, already met, this morning in another house or in the streets of Siena, or when he visited the headquarters of the *contrada* of the Wave, or even later, in the chapel of the Forest, during the blessing of the horse.

Countless introductions, countless handshakes, as if everyone knew everyone else.

It's Siena, a small city, that has this effect on him, he thinks. But he knows that, were he to run the binoculars over the crowd framed by the circle of palaces, he would recognize each one of these fifty thousand molecules; for each one he would seek its pre-existing pigeonhole.

Yes, everyone around him has a secret, a subtle, elastic secret that stretches and stretches without ever snapping, like the long procrastination of the historic procession. Will it be the race, then, that decides matters, that blows it all sky-high? Is this then the meaning (the secret) of the Palio of Siena, at least for him? A revelation awaits him. The final crowning victory of one of the many hypotheses that have been competing within him for the last three days.

*

The evening of the fourteenth, after dinner, coffee was served on the terrace in front of the villa, and Avvocato Maggioni, contemplating the black creepers that entwined arabesque adornments over the facade and around the windows, three of which were lit up on different floors, had the impression that he was discovering a coded message aimed at him, the key to which he did not yet possess. It was then that he felt he understood his own perplexities and was able to give a name to his own uneasiness. It's a ciphered villa, he thought. But since this was just an expression, he forced himself to be more precise, more specific.

Above all, there was a sense of unfamiliarity, which needed to be subdivided in turn, or rather, broken into fractions. Twenty per cent should obviously be attributed to the initial error of the wrong road taken, to that early disconcertment caused by the hailstorm. A clear fifteen per cent to social disorientation, these not being the kind of people Valeria and he usually mixed with. Another twenty per cent to their being plunged into the fiery passions and complicated rules of the Palio: a race, when one thought about it, that was peculiarly singular, peculiarly exotic. And then, at the very least, forty per cent to Puddu, what with his biting, his screaming and his death. Which amounted to ninety-five per cent.

There remained five per cent to be understood, to be sorted out.

But it was perhaps in these two concepts that the key to everything lay.

Did not the real discomfort, the real sense of unfamiliarity, come directly from there, from this gradually growing urge, from this insistent suspicion that behind every slightest thing, behind every person, word or gesture, even every object (even the dog) there lay something to be understood?

Life wasn't like that. In life things were what they were; they happened because they happened, without all this fuss. You tried to park in the centre of town, you bought a packet of cigarettes, drank a glass of beer, watched television. What else was there to say or to discover about such events? Nothing.

Whereas here the superficial had disappeared; the villa (it was in this sense that it could be described as ciphered) was merely a false bottom or secret compartment; it too was an alias, like everything in Siena.

Avvocato Maggioni was seized by an acute nostalgia for simplicity, for the soothing obviousness of an evening at home with his legs stretched out towards the television – and he scrutinized the outline of the roof in search of a friendly aerial. But it was too dark to make one out, if there was one. And to tell the truth, mentally going over all the rooms he had been in, he realized that he hadn't seen the familiar object in any of them.

"You don't have a television anywhere, do you?" he asked Ginevra, who was walking by with a shawl for Elisabetta.

"No. Why?"

"No reason. Just to know."

She gave him a pat on the cheek with two light fingers and walked away.

There you go, thought the lawyer, she's given me a pat on the cheek. A good thing. A great thing. Why can't I take it for what it is? Instead, his obsession with sorting things out was already there, like a Bengal tiger: a) cheek pat of the carefree kind; b) cheek pat of the affectionate kind; c) of the promising kind; d) of the casual kind; et cetera.

Just take your wretched cheek pat, he told himself, and think no more about it.

He looked at the moon as it rose behind a hill, and started up again:

a) moon of the romantic kind (and, on cue, Valeria, dressed in white for the soirée, got to her feet and walked towards the Italian-style garden in Guidobaldo's company);

b) moon of the meteorological kind (and, on cue, Ascanio and Elisabetta started talking about tomorrow's weather);

c) moon of the rural kind (and, on cue, Ranieri and Salimbeni began a conversation on harvests and Green Europe and American agricultural surpluses);

d) moon of the sinister kind (and, on cue, he was reminded of the scream of agony of the previous night).

With this fixation on "kinds", it was impossible to live; nothing stood for itself, nothing seemed authentic or real, including Paolino up there, among his fake beans, his fake flies. That was how the villa's cipher worked.

It was, he reflected, a contradictory scheme, a double-edged sword, which took away with one hand what it gave you with the other. It added fifty per cent of mystery but the other fifty per cent collapsed into banality. Each secret door opened onto a scene that had already been viewed. Each magic word evoked a cliché. Each unforeseen development ended up in the foreseeable. Each emotional outburst hurled you into soppiness. False bottom? Yes, but full of wastepaper.

Who wouldn't have had a crisis, falling into a situation like this? But the very word "crisis" here had resonances of a cultural, divulgatory kind that were enough to make him sick. It was only Valeria, wholly absorbed in her "romantic" kind, who could fail to notice anything.

"I'm going to bed, I'm a bit tired," he announced to the others. "Goodnight, everyone."

A moon of the drowsy kind accompanied him to the loggia.

But during the night, when someone woke him by gently stroking the cheek that had been patted, outside the window he saw a moon of the amorous kind. Then the orb merged into the passionate kind, then to the kind for adults only, then to the exhausted kind, the sentimental kind, the incredulous kind.

"But why with me?"

"Why not."

"You're too beautiful, I don't deserve you."

"Take it as a gift. Now I have to go."

"You're a fairy. It's all a dream. Tell me it's not a dream."

"Don't be silly. Ciao, see you tomorrow."

Instead, he saw her less than half an hour later. That gift or dream, whichever it was, had aroused hunger of the most prosaic type in him, and finally he decided to go down to the ground floor, stirred by very specific advertising images: cheeses, cold meats, crackers, snacks, even just peanuts. Flailing around in the dark among unfindable light switches and unrecognizable doors, he opened one of the latter and found himself with one foot inside the Indian Room, lit up by its massive chandelier.

Ginevra raised two totally inexpressive eyes to him, as if she had never seen him before; almost, indeed, as if she didn't see him. She and the others – Ascanio, Elisabetta, Guidobaldo, Ranieri and Salimbeni – were sitting in a silent circle on those rigid red chairs that looked like so many little thrones, and the portraits on the wall in some way multiplied the assembly.

"Oh, sorry," said Avvocato Maggioni. What else could he say, with twelve eyes trained on him?

He withdrew, confused and puzzled. Sure, it was a group of Sienese who were directly involved in the Palio, and Puddu's death had without doubt greatly complicated matters for them. But four o'clock (more or less) in the morning seemed a rather unusual hour to get together to discuss things. And why in that room? The question of the six of them seemed a difficult kind to define.

XVII

The next day, 15 August, was mainly a day of pauses and repetitions. The sun resumed its place in the cloudless sky, the scrub stretched out again on the hills, the villa recovered its rooms, staircases, corridors, among which the lawyer found his way with a sense of almost bored familiarity. Once again, the boar's head. Once again, the stone staircase and the tenebrous entrance hall. Once again, the billiard room, with Ascanio playing (pok pok pok) his usual game. Once again, the library, the Indian Room, the Sodoma Room, in which the Neapolitan magistrate had reinstalled himself. The same suit as yesterday, the same moustache, the same gesticulatory vivacity, the same white cigarette holder which periodically scattered ash over his jacket.

Even Puddu came back. His oblique and triumphant sneer, photographed after a victory, filled the middle of a page of *La Nazione*, full of news about him and containing an emotional statement from Torcicollo, his great rival. His death was attributed to a generic "collapse", and there was no reference to an autopsy or to the enquiries under way.

Throughout the day the tortuous family relations among the inhabitants of the villa returned to the fore several times, with the addition, thanks to the contribution of the two new arrivals from Rome, of another fifty per cent at least of combinations and complications. Ranieri's father, famously gay, had adopted the son of a former cook of Elisabetta, who was actually the fruit of an adulterous relationship between a brother of Ascanio and a sister of Salimbeni, this latter later committing suicide in Paris, and whose husband, ruined by gambling, had been obliged to sell the Rombaie to an uncle of...

On several occasions Avvocato Maggioni had to invent pretexts to get away from revelations of this kind, which nonetheless threw a new light on the unusual meeting in the Indian Room.

Had the six of them really been talking about the Palio last night? Or had the two from Rome come to negotiate some intricate question of inheritance, the transfer or division of some large property, maybe of the villa itself?

It was a fact that the economy, along with politics, represented eighty-five per cent net of their utterances, which always seemed to begin with the words "if the dollar" or "the latest amendment". And yet their presence here remained unclear, their "kind" uncertain. They behaved like a couple set apart; they had not relaxed or made themselves comfortable, they had not divested themselves of their dark-blue silk suits, their city shoes, their sober ties. It was not a holiday or festive occasion for them.

Valeria clearly admired them, hanging on their lips even if she didn't understand a word they said, showing the same compunction that she did when reading the "serious" columns of her weekly magazines; but then, two minutes later, she would move on to something else – to Guidobaldo, alias the man of destiny, alias Prince Charming, alias *o sole mio*.

Gossamer gazes, whipped-cream smiles, ciao-ciao waves from windows, fluttering frissons as if wafted from one dragonfly to another, cheek-by-cheek strolls with their feet barely touching the ground along the path that led to the greenhouses and stables, whispered conversations, what I feel for you what I don't feel for you, let's enjoy the moment let's not enjoy the moment.

Poor Valeria, who all the while had to strain her ears, as with a simultaneous translation, to catch the doubt of all doubts, the suspicion of all suspicions: does he love me for myself or is he only interested in my body (alias...)?

At a fork in the road the lawyer lost sight of the two romantic figurines, on their way towards immense truths and cosmic idiocies. As he walked back up a low hill covered in bushes, he ran into Ginevra and Elisabetta, who were coming down it, swinging tennis rackets.

"Did you want to play a game?" Ginevra asked him.

"No, no, I haven't played in years."

"That's bad, tennis is an all-round sport, like swimming," Elisabetta said reprovingly. And she started a lecture of the calisthenic kind, on the need to keep fit after a certain age, on the metabolism, reflexes, breathing…

"Yes, it's true, but in Milan…" said the lawyer, looking at Ginevra and hoping she would help him out.

But Ginevra must have been of the calisthenic kind herself this morning, because she began to fill him in on the virtues of a low-mineral water recommended by Ascanio. "He knocks back litres and litres every day," she explained, "and says that they swish through the system like cars on the motorway, purifying it wonderfully." She then went on to talk to Elisabetta about the new dishwasher that they had ended up ordering, because the old one was almost rusted through and the Filipino servants kept complaining about it. "Apparently it's a very new kind of steel, much more…"

"Oh yes, and anyway it's a very good brand, Salimbeni's sister has got one, well, actually, she's got two: one for…"

A ridiculous and unsettling deduction imposed itself on Avvocato Maggioni on that gentle slope as he absorbed the scents of the Mediterranean scrub and the sight of a landscape immortalized in a thousand leaflets and a hundred documentaries. The two women were actually dubbed; everything that everyone said was dubbed: they moved their lips, but the words that emerged came from a hidden speaker reading a script.

It's the sun that's having this effect on me, he thought as the women moved away, still conversing. It's the effect of the August sun.

He wiped his handkerchief over his brow, which was not sweaty. He tried to breathe in and out, to flex his arms. All fine, even without tennis and low-mineral water.

It was an effect of the villa, then. Once again it was the villa that was imprisoning him, conditioning him with its futile, repetitive incantations, interposing its invisible veil, its ciphered screen, between him and life.

I must get away from here, I must escape, he thought, rotating his shoulders energetically as if trying to extricate himself from a twisted sheet.

How far could the radius of the villa's influence extend? To the end of the scrubland? To Siena? To the Melegnano tollbooth? To the cathedral of his own city?

He reached the tennis court, threatened on all four sides by advancing lines of weeds, its dark surface scored by feebly pallid lines as if marking the outline of an obliterated temple. On the further side, beyond a rusty and gashed wire fence, ran a hedge of enormous oleanders which, in the disorder of their wild old age, threw up great flowery splashes of pink and red.

From that direction came the croaking, rhythmical sound of a guitar, and the lawyer realized that until then the musical "kind" had been absent, among the many suggested to him. There it is, he thought with a sort of satisfaction.

To avert the risk of tearing his shirt amid the oleanders and the remains of the wire fence, he walked around the court and found himself gazing at the unexpected (but foreseeable) swimming pool, this too degraded, worn away at the edges, the water murky and strewn with leaves, twigs and a few storm-scattered red flowers.

A girl of about ten was dancing barefoot on the concrete trampoline to the sound of a little radio which hung from the belt of her jeans. Seeing the lawyer, she did not stop but rather began to thrash about even more frantically, shaking her head and whirling her arms as if she were trying to keep afloat in the rhythmic sea of sound.

"Who are you?"

"Barabesi Cinzia," the girl panted, still dancing. "The gardener's granddaughter."

"You're not afraid of falling in?"

"No, I can swim. I'm also taking sailing lessons."

In some way she managed to make the syllables match the beat of the music, and they came out like a kind of senseless rhythmical song, amid crashing drum rolls and explosive guitar chords.

"My grandpa went with the carabinieri into the scrubland," she sang urgently.

Was that the Nescafé man, who had now gone over into detective stories?

The lawyer now saw the gnarled old man emerging from the scrub, which began twenty yards or so away, preceding the marshal, another officer and the Neapolitan magistrate in shirtsleeves. This latter took out the empty cigarette holder he had been clutching between his teeth and greeted him with a great shout of "My dear Avvocato!", as if across the whole Bay of Naples.

"We've been carrying out a little inspection," the magistrate explained, "to try to see where the deceased went walking the other night." He carefully screwed a cigarette into the holder and lit it with gusto. "You know, I had to refrain from lighting it while in the scrub. In the summer there's always the risk of fires."

"And what did you find?"

"Not much, not much. The ground is still wet from the rain, and the prints of his studs can be followed clearly enough to a small clearing. But they end there."

"Wouldn't it have been better to do this inspection yesterday?"

The magistrate flung wide his arms. "My dear Avvocato, what can I say?"

"There must be the traces of his walk back, no? Pointing in the opposite direction, I mean."

"No sign of them. He must have returned by another path, which has now been trampled by a herd of boars. And there are also horses' hoofprints, it's all a bit of a mess... But what a lovely radio this young lady has," he said, putting his hand on Cinzia's head.

"It's an Ichiko 140, it's an Ichiko 140, it's even got frequency modulation!" warbled the girl, and she skipped away, turning the volume up to its maximum.

"Sweet little girl," said the magistrate, turning to the old man. "Your granddaughter?"

The old man shook his head, growing serious. "She's not really my granddaughter," he explained. "Years ago, my sister was a wardrobe mistress at the villa when Signor Ascanio's wife called her up and confided to her that a niece of her husband had been... you get me... *compromised* by Signorino Guidobaldo's brother..."

With bowed head Avvocato Maggioni walked away from the inane, persistent dubbing.

*

For the rest of the day he tried to keep away from the implacable mechanism that falsified and rendered meaningless everything in turn. But he himself was now an accomplice of the alternations, trapped in the grid of criss-crossing variations.

He:

cleaned his teeth with a toothpaste containing Frigol O.

offered Scattomints on various occasions to one or other of the people there.

contemplated yet again the portraits of the tiger hunter and of Violante of Bavaria.

couldn't avoid seeing two men in overalls unloading a brand-new dishwasher from a brand-new Mercedes van.

passed through an opaque interval of sleep, but when he woke, he saw from his window the Filipino woman pouring Puppy Chef into the dog bowl.

couldn't help wondering with a yawn whether, after all, she might have been the one who had killed Puddu, with some East Asian poison.

saw, yet again, the Neapolitan magistrate pulling up in his car (metallic blue Fiat 131), smoking as he did so, and wondered how Puddu had really died, and when they would hear the results of the autopsy.

followed with his eyes the Valeria–Guidobaldo couple, wandering obliviously around the boxwoods and flower beds of the Italian-style garden ("our love has a future our love has no future").

followed with his eyes the Ranieri–Salimbeni duo passing in front of the window of the billiard room ("if the German mark", "as a consequence of the Legislative Decree").

followed the already-seen sun passively as it slipped below the already-seen horizon.

heard Ascanio and the old gardener commenting on the sunset and forecasting tomorrow's weather, while Cinzia climbed onto the balustrade, and, suspended over the void, started up her frantic song and dance routine despite rebukes from her fake grandfather.

Then the aperitifs reappeared (a trolley loaded with bottles, bowls of snacks, olives, boar sausages), the Filipino man reappeared to announce dinner; the conversation on the Palio and the *contrade* and the rules and Torcicollo started up again (a little further on? a little further back?); the abnormal excrescence of the family (what family?) began to spread again (from what point? up to what point?), extending its tentacles of cousins, sisters, husbands, adulteries, abortions, divorces and adoptions.

The moon reproduced itself, at first effortfully but then, with a sudden leap, hanging high in the sky, and Avvocato Maggioni reconsidered the facade of the villa in its deceptive glimmering light, the rigid scheme of the windows, the ramified snare of the creepers.

He thought: it's an image of my malaise; there's a sort of conspiracy trying to crush my status as an average man.

He thought: this thought is as dubbed, emphatic and empty as everything else; now I have to monitor not only what I do and say, but even what I think. Who would have thought it?

He thought futilely: Christ, what's happening to me?

The lawyer took his leave of the circle of dark silhouettes on the glimmering gravel, went back up to his room and cleaned his teeth again.

In the night, as he had expected, Ginevra came back, and he went back to uttering the dubbed sentences that rose uncontrollably to his lips. There was, it seemed, a shade of obedience in everything he did. Is this what they want from me? he thought.

He fell asleep thinking, obediently, of his relationship or non-relationship with Ginevra, of his relationship or non-relationship with life.

XVIII

On the morning of 16 August, after a hasty breakfast, Avvocato Maggioni was thrust hurriedly into the dark Opel, which set off at once for Siena. In the excitement and general confusion the problem of how to recover their car and luggage after the Palio had remained unsolved, whether they should return to the villa or stay and sleep in the city, whether the Filipino would see to everything or whether Paolino could be entrusted with the whole matter the next day.

But the alternatives of the Palio made all other alternatives irrelevant, and even Valeria, electrified by the imminence of the great challenge, by the dilemma of who's going to win who's not going to win, had reduced her habitual dilemma of what shall I wear what shan't I wear to the bare minimum.

She was in the car with Guidobaldo. Ginevra was given a lift by Ascanio and Elisabetta.

Not a word about the race was exchanged between

Ranieri and Salimbeni during the journey. The lawyer, who was sitting in the front, next to the driver, began to suspect that the two were not Sienese at all; they seemed more like two politicians of anonymous provenance, on their way to Siena for some conference or important meeting.

The three cars all met up inside a palazzo in the centre of the city, amid gothic precipices and a colonnade lined with Etruscan sarcophagi and truncated memorial stones. A public building? A museum?

But during the short journey the lawyer had moved, so to speak, in reverse; those miles of hills had opened horizons of rebellious indifference. He no longer asked himself anything, he felt below any kind of curiosity. Why don't they just leave me here, among these Etruscan ashes, he thought.

Walking through the streets with the others, he found himself eyeing a small tavern wedged between an ogival earthenware arch and a grim studded door, or a squalid wine bar supporting four storeys of square medieval stone blocks, and he imagined slowing his pace, getting left behind, surreptitiously slipping into those dark retreats and spending the rest of the day all alone, expunged at last from every race, every discomfort, every scheme, every mystery. But one didn't do such things.

Banners, flags, standards and drapes with the colours of the seventeen *contrade* covered Siena, its windows, balconies, shopfronts, cornices, bicycles and motor-bikes; and the roads closed to traffic were shaken by the incessant, impetuous tramping of footsteps coming from all over and going all over, with firm purposefulness.

"What's the matter, don't you like it?" said Ginevra, taking him by the arm.

"No, on the contrary. It's just that I'm a bit tired."

She smiled, pointing at two small boys at the far end of a courtyard who were tossing up and catching two banners of the Tortoise in mid-air. "They start very young."

"And don't the girls do it?"

"No, there are no women in the historic procession."

"Pity. I'd love to see you parading in costume."

"Dressed as what?"

As madonna? As fairy? Or as fawn, filly, gazelle?

"Maybe naked," he blurted out.

"Come along, come to the church, let's go to the cathedral and see what the Drappellone is like."

They clambered up narrow lanes, but the great door of the cathedral was obstructed by Frankish, Longobard, Helvetian, Saxon, Gothic, Britannic tourists, and in any case Ginevra was soon spotting, greeting, embracing and introducing him to at least a dozen people (a man in a tartan jacket, a woman all in turquoise, a shirtless lad with thick glasses) while Elisabetta, Guidobaldo and all the others were doing exactly the same with dozens of other people in various points of the square.

The lawyer recognized the Neapolitan magistrate, who was cleaving his way laboriously through the crowd followed by his family, and turned away from him. "There are too many people, let's leave."

"Come on, I'll take you to see the *Maestà* by Duccio at least."

But there, too, they found a dense, massive invasion of Franks and Longobards, and the great painting itself, gleaming in the dim light, struck him as overcrowded with angels and saints.

They walked, getting lost and finding their way again, in the steeply sloping labyrinth that was Siena, amid the tolling of bells, joyous choruses, shouts, shrieks, and always that breathless rush of bodies from every corner to every other corner. Laminated or nylon emblems of the city flaunted their black-and-white chessboards on all sides, but whichever way they moved – sideways, forwards or backwards – they never emerged into the Piazza del Campo, which could only be intuited, like the depression of a lake beyond a ring of hills.

"But wasn't there a final trial run this morning?"

"Yes, the *provaccia*. But it's late now."

"Better that way. I prefer the real race."

Ginevra looked at him with a slight (indecipherable?) smile. "You're right," she said approvingly.

But Ascanio and Elisabetta deviated towards the Campo and were swallowed up by the clamouring, pressing torrent. Ranieri and Salimbeni disappeared as well, swallowed up by an entrance hall where a votive lamp burned. Ahead of them Valeria and Guidobaldo entered a cake shop, and re-emerged behind them with two huge ice creams.

"Should I buy a scarf of your *contrada*?"

"Of the Forest? Of course not, that's ridiculous, you're not Sienese."

"Well, for solidarity."

"Forget it, what do you care about the Forest?"

Amid a flurry of new embraces and new introductions, they visited the rooms of the Capitana Contrada of the Wave, where, together with other precious mementos, the heraldic dolphins glowed palely, reproduced on ancient metals, ancient papers and ancient silks along the walls and in showcases.

Many wore scarves with undulating white and blue stripes around their necks, and – for an instant, like a hazy movie still – the image of Puddu's corpse in the library flashed before the lawyer. What had been the colour of that scarf that had vanished so quickly? Impossible to remember. Today, 16 August, it was already impossible to be certain that the now remote memento had ever existed.

They all met up again in the house of some friends, and from the balconies, each of them holding a plate of cold meat, they found themselves unexpectedly looking out over Siena, a city of roofs laid out by a crazed Euclid. And yet that fantastic collection of angles, slopes, superimpositions and inclinations was firmly homogeneous and gave no indication of streets, squares or alleys. The crowds had disappeared, the population was nowhere to be seen; from here all the *contrade* appeared equally suppressed, dead and buried beneath the compact expanse of roof tiles. A hermetic city. A ciphered city, no less.

And suppose there *was* nobody down there any more? the lawyer asked himself. And suppose this were the last secret, the ungraspable allusion, the insistent cross reference.

He was on the point of leaving them all and going back down to check, but the large and small groups all got in his way, ensnaring him, offering him salad and low-mineral water; like brambles in the forest they held him up with conversations on the weather, sailing (an all-round sport), the Swiss franc, Puddu, cars, fridges, dogs, olives, boars, shampoos and other vain ardours.

The lawyer wearily slipped his hand into his pocket and was about to pull out Scattomints and offer them around when a drum roll escaped from the clutch of the roofs and the whole mass of guests stiffened and rushed towards rooms further inside. He, too, was swept along with the others (but it was Ginevra who steered him; the lawyer had a lightning-flash memory of Dante being guided by Virgil and then by Beatrice), and he finally found himself leaning listlessly on the sill of a long window high above an alleyway.

Then something changed.

But it was not Ginevra, it was not the precise information being offered by Ascanio (the *comparse* of the *contrade* were beginning to make their way towards their respective chapels for the ceremony of the blessing of the horse), it was not the helmets and the broad caps, all closely packed together, nor the costumes thrown into relief by the leprous walls of the narrow alley, nor the powerful parade horse with its statuesque rider; it was not the banners, the pageboys, the children shouting and leaping around the *bàrbero* as it stomped its hooves nervously on the cobblestones; it was not the anachronistic atmosphere nor the theatrical enchantment of the occasion; it was the sound of the drum (planned? calculated? tossed there by *la sorte?*) that finally sent the shiver of the Palio running down Avvocato Maggioni's spine.

That military summons was for him; that fabulous drum roll was bidding him come down from his centuries of lethargy, announcing that only down there, where the close-packed Euclidean roofs finally loosened their clutch around the great empty space of the shell, only on the Piazza del Campo could the deciphering perhaps be accomplished.

*

With the others, the lawyer ran down the stony steps and streets; with the others, he found himself barricaded inside a minuscule temple where the *bàrbero* quivered and stamped the ground in front of the altar, while the priest exhorted it to win for its *contrada* and solemnly raised his arm to bless it. With the others, he exulted when the bowels of the beast "showed disrespect" (a sure sign of victory) towards the sanctity of the place and a sudden stench of the stables wafted around the sacred images and furnishings.

The omen is for me, thought the lawyer with a sour sense of payback. I'm going to win as well.

Then, the six of them dispersed among the palaces and balconies. Guidobaldo carried off Valeria, Ginevra led him to a gloomy backstreet and then up a staircase with broad, flaking stairs, floor after floor, to a door guarded by a butler, and through rooms and salons amid men and women and handshakes, all the way to a window, outside of which the great shell magically opened up – the navel, the heart of the enigma.

Here is the cipher, Avvocato Maggioni intuited triumphantly, here I will know.

He embraced Ginevra and began his long surveillance.

XIX

So: the standard-bearers of all the *contrade*, lined up beneath the Palazzo Pubblico, all hurl their gaudy missiles skywards, the multicoloured silks unfurl and the heraldic bestiary of dolphins and panthers, giraffes and she-wolves takes wing for an instant, then folds in on itself and plummets to the ground.

It's the last flag display, the last salute of the *comparse*. The standard-bearers then go and take their posts in the special raised tribune where the other extras are sitting in unexpectedly close, compact rows.

It's like a fuse, thinks Avvocato Maggioni, a slow fuse that has been sizzling for over an hour, yard by yard, around the ring of tuff in preparation for the final explosion.

So: an unbearable silence falls upon the Campo, upon the entire city. The spectators on the balconies and at the windows are more tightly packed than ever; the spectators are suddenly doubled in number, the heads tripled. The American woman clutches at him from the right, thrust there by urgent insinuations; on his left Ginevra nestles even more compactly under his arm; sweaty bodies pressing from behind push him against the windowsill; hands are resting on his shoulders, wafts of warm breath tickle his neck.

But Maggioni barely notices these crushing contacts. Melded into the crowd, he has somehow become immaterial, bodiless, elevated into a superior sphere of pure and utter expectation. And at the same time it is as if his faculties have become fantastically multiplied, as if all the eyes, all the ears and lungs, diaphragms, hearts, pores and nerves gathered here together depend on him alone. He feels annulled and at the same time collectivized.

He is pervaded by a vertiginous sense of simultaneity. He sees the attendants, who, armed with spades, are rushing to cancel the thick traces left by men, horses and oxen on the racetrack, the parallel furrows left by the *carroccio*. And at the same time, he sees the deserted streets of Siena, he perceives a tiny percentage of exceptions, an old man with Parkinson's disease sitting at the far end of a dark kitchen, a nun praying inside a large, empty church, two lovers embracing in a shadowy alleyway. But it doesn't escape him that on the Torre del Mangia the hole in the quadrant of the great clock now frames a human face, a perfect miniature on white enamel; he is aware of the restless horses inside the courtyard of the podestà, each one tied to its own numbered pillar, and of the jockeys as they nervously pull on their racing jerseys and pick up their helmets with the colours of the *contrada*; he makes out the starter, a young man dressed in brown with his tie askew, waving his arms around on his dais (which is also known as "Verrocchio"), while in front of him someone is checking the device that sets off the firecracker known as the *mortaletto* and other attendants are stretching the two *canapi* across the track to mark out the narrow space where the horses will line up for the starting signal; and he hears the Deputies of the Feast confabulating, over there on the judges' stand, where the Palio is displayed, as they prepare the last intervention of *la sorte* and get ready to open the double cylinder in which the starting order is sealed.

In this teeming navel of the universe that Siena has become, no one breathes (apart from a few insignificant exceptions: a fat shopkeeper who has reached the first floor of a medieval house in Via Bandini and is preparing to confront a creditor; a little girl who is blowing on her doll's minuscule bowl to cool imaginary soup). No muscle moves in this petrified Pompeian mass, in this concentrated Etruscan necropolis, of which Avvocato Maggioni is a part and the whole.

*

Fourteen swallows flicker over the vast catalepsy of the crowd.

A white cat leaps among the merlons of the Palazzo Pubblico.

Blast of the *mortaletto.*

The first horse, already mounted, moves towards the "grand entrance", the jockey (it's the Eagle) bends down to receive his ox-sinew whip from a traffic officer, emerges, swaying, on the track, and, amid a simultaneity that is now vociferous, banner-waving and delirious, Avvocato Maggioni's eyes follow the ten *bàrberi* as they move towards the ropes; he follows the gestures of the starter as he receives an envelope, breaks its seal, opens it and starts to shout the starting order.

"Seashell!"

"Wave!"

"She-wolf!"

"Giraffe!"

A roar greets each name, merges into the next one, ends up tempestuously covering the roll call, while one by one the horses pass through the gap of the first rope, docile or reluctant, restrained or stimulated by the jockeys who grip the single rein with seriousness, nonchalance, pride, resolution or ostentatious laziness, depending on their temperament or on the image they want to project of themselves – old foxes, bastards, skunks, hyenas, crooks, thieves, wretches, as the whole piazza (the quality of the vocal rumble has changed) is now calling them.

There they are between the ropes, exchanging last-minute confirmations of alliance or neutrality, offering themselves up for the final shameless betrayal, for the last crucial bribe. And their brusque conventional signs, never more than two or three fingers flicked forwards, their threatening or malignant mimes, their words spat forth through barely moving lips, are matched by the ceaseless agitation of the horses, the trembling of muscles, the neurotic stamping at the ground, the twists, retreats and sudden forward jerks.

In that confused swirling of heads, hooves, backs, chests, tails, necks, manes, the number of animals between the ropes seems to Avvocato Maggioni to be far more than ten – or rather nine, since the tenth (the Panther) remains outside, a few yards further back; from there he will dart forwards one instant before the others, this short starting run compensating for the disadvantage of setting out from the most external position.

Insults and incitements are raining down on all the jockeys, but it is the Panther, as he now slips between the ropes illegitimately, as if dragged by his black horse, that draws upon himself the most ferocious sarcastic quips, the most obscene invitations, the most blistering curses and exhortations, because this is Torcicollo,

171

the great rival of Ganascino on the track and in dirty work – he, too, a cunning bastard, he, too, the crook of all crooks, the scum of the earth, so that his innocent, impotent air, as he weaves his way amid the spasmodic contractions of his colleagues, fools no one, least of all the starter, who angrily rebukes him, drives him out, sends him back to his starting position.

With an acrobatic twisting of his shoulder and of the whole of his right arm, the lawyer manages to pick up the binoculars that the American woman has laid down in front of her, and then to raise them to his eyes to get an idea of what this Torcicollo looks like – he, too, perhaps a woman-biter or God knows what else.

And the lenses reveal to him, greatly magnified, a Danish beer can poised over two lips.

Ah yes, he thinks.

He then shifts the binoculars – with difficulty, because he is holding them with one hand.

There now appears a small boy sitting on his father's shoulders, in the act of unwrapping a stick of chewing gum.

Yes, of course.

The lawyer manages to extricate his elbow and laboriously rotate his wrist, but someone shoves him from behind, makes him lose his aim, and the image now captured by the lenses (the numerous, too numerous horses between the ropes) is grey and blurred; the focus wheel must have shifted. With the index finger and thumb of the hand holding the binoculars, the lawyer struggles to bring the confused scene before him into focus, but the convulsed jostling of horses and jockeys remains full of shifting shadows as diaphanous horse-backs collide with inconsistent chests, evanescent manes brush against milky heads, and Avvocato Maggioni is about to give up, is about to replace the binoculars acrobatically on the sill, when.

When no, he thinks.

It's not possible.

The jockey he momentarily glimpsed slips from his field of view, and the lawyer gives a brutal start, shoves Ginevra backwards, shoves the American woman backwards, shakes off the whole crowd of Siena, and with his two hands finally free firmly grips the binoculars, aims them at the ropes, seeking…

And he sees him. He discovers him, flushes him out – for one second, from the nebulous muddle, he extracts the black moustache, teeth and memorable sneer of Puddu.

"What's the matter?" asks Ginevra with her lips only, because the persistent bawling of the piazza prevents any other sound from getting through. "What did you see?"

But it's not a question, the lawyer realizes. Ginevra is staring at him without curiosity and without smiling. Ginevra knows. Ginevra knew.

"Nothing," he says with his lips.

They gaze at each other.

You should have understood, say Ginevra's eyes, in which a vague, hasty expression of apology can now be read.

But I did understand, lie Avvocato Maggioni's eyes, out of politeness, submissive docility.

Whereas in fact he had only vaguely grasped the coincidence between the six suppressed *contrade* and the six people of the villa gathered in the dead of night in the Indian Room; he had vaguely sensed their "diversity", vaguely intuited the thread, the impalpable intrigue woven by them among the other rougher intrigues and threads of the last three days.

Was it *this*, then, that would not let itself be "understood", "sorted out"?

Was this the cipher, the secret?

Avvocato Maggioni knows that the wait is not over; he feels the other suspicions, the other hypotheses, the other possibilities, kicking and thrashing restlessly between his own ropes as a logical man, as an average man.

Three days of doubts, he thinks, will be disentangled in three circuits of the track. It will be the Palio of Revelations, all yet to be run. One will prevail.

XX

The piazza is a hysterical funnel, the very circle of the palazzi seems too fragile for this explosive hubbub, the ancient walls could be torn apart like paper at any second; and the starter is flailing around with the desperation of one who, all alone, has to avert the impending catastrophe.

But the horses recoil, writhe and squirm before the rope, the line-up forms and immediately breaks up, recomposes itself, collapses because the Seashell pushes past the She-wolf, the Eagle slips in between the Wave and Giraffe, the Porcupine changes places with the Tower, in a continual reshuffling that could go on forever, because among the ten (or rather, nine) competitors between the ropes, the lawyer now senses (and he is not the only one!), deduces the opaque interference, the simultaneous presence of six (or rather, five) other equine and human shapes, the horses and jockeys of the dead *contrade*. And further back, poised for the running start, the black *bàrbero* of Torcicollo is flanked, as by a duplicated image, by a coincidental and implacable spectre – that of Puddu, mounted on his phantom *bàrbero*, he, too, poised to seize the decisive moment.

Neither of the two moves when the intolerable tension urges all the other jockeys, of the living as well as the dead *contrade*, to burst past the rope and gallop off headlong, whips raised.

The *mortaletto* sounds to call them back.

It was a false start, and the two champions did not fall for it. They share an identical sneer as they wheel round to flaunt their superior, icy coolness, while the other competitors gradually make their way back, despondent and enervated, to the starting line.

An angry, treacherous sobriety hangs over the piazza: it's a pause that will not last long; here and there re-inflated lungs resound, recharged throats recreate the deafening choral unity, raising it to an even more raucous and frenzied level. The starter's face is scarlet; his arms repeat the same vain gestures of command, faster and faster. The horses, too, accelerate their shoves and kicks, their twisted jerks and capricious archings.

Then once again they all rush forwards uncontrollably.

Avvocato Maggioni remains icily cool in his place, like the two champions, who have not budged this time either.

The *mortaletto* sounds.

The crowd's disappointed howl swells and subsides again, the mortifying return procession is replicated, Torcicollo and the accompanying shade of Puddu keep up their display of gloating scorn, and the same air of strangled suspense presses down on the piazza once again.

Now the starter's face is very pale. The jockeys' faces, deformed by irrepressible grimaces, are also very pale at the resumption of the dance of the line-up, which no longer has anything elegant or calculated about it but is just a contracted series of bumps and bounces.

Amid this angry and static melee Avvocato Maggioni is struck by a sense of frozen quiet, a presage of eternity. The piazza falls silent. The swallows seem turned to stone on the cornices. The incessant trembling of the old man with Parkinson's disease is momentarily suspended. The little girl's spoon as she feeds her doll has halted in mid-air. Valeria and Guidobaldo are statues on their balcony, and Ascanio, Elisabetta, Ranieri and Salimbeni, at whatever window or balcony they are perched, have stopped talking and moving too. By his side, Ginevra herself, the sinuous ex-gazelle, ex-deer, ex-cat, has the silent hardness of a fossil. On the Torre del Mangia the face of the solitary spectator is forever embedded in the clock face, which will show the same time for ever and ever.

The lawyer is not surprised.

All the colours crumble and flake away from things; a grey mesh swathes them like a diagonal hailstorm.

The lawyer waits patiently, soaked in sweat, suffocated by everything around him.

He imagines (or sees?) a naked girl in the freshness of a shower as she soaps herself with Camay.

He sees (or imagines?) a small boy pouring Fanta orangeade into his mouth.

Of course, he thinks.

From this interruption, the Palio returns as if amplified and enraged, slamming the eardrums, flooding the retinas with dazzling colours, at the precise instant in which Torcicollo hurls himself into the gap of the opening gallop, head to head with the spectral *bàrbero* of his great rival.

Each of the fifty thousand throats invokes the name of its own *contrada*.

"Viper!" invokes Ginevra's throat. "Viper!"

This time there is no firecracker summons to return, and from her balcony Valeria sees the impetuous mass rushing towards her unhesitatingly, the horses' lean bodies straining to their utmost, the jockeys bent forwards intently. She feels part of the race herself, leaping, quivering, racing, clutching at the reins of the balustrade together with them all.

Guidobaldo (whose presence, strange stiffness and impassivity she senses beside her) is right: the only thing comparable with this race is a great orgasm, a mad orgasm, a world-ending one (as her friend Ornella would say), intensified by those two false starts that almost (she would say) drove her mad.

Ten yards. Twenty yards.

Amid the explosive jubilation Valeria catches a voice emitting inarticulate screams (it's her own) when two jockeys close to the rope exchange furious whiplashes and one of them (she recognizes him, it's the Seashell!) already loses ground, slips towards the rear of the galloping pack, but at once he jerks up his arm to block another competitor, who, whirling his whip in turn, tries to avoid getting overtaken by a fourth (it's the Forest!) rival.

Thirty yards.

And from yard to yard a rapid carousel of images and fractions of images whirls by, like cards shuffled by a prodigious conjurer. But the real prodigy is that Valeria doesn't miss a single one; she infallibly records and recomposes every single variation and superimposition, the crimson red of the Tower flanking the white and blue of the Wave, the black and white of the She-wolf overtaking the red and white of the Giraffe, the golden yellow of the Eagle holding its own against the green and orange of the Forest, the red and blue of the Panther moving up menacingly from the outside, menaced in turn by the green and yellow of the Viper.

Stride by stride the pack gains ground, and in the foreground Valeria perceives Guidobaldo's hands clutching, like her own, at the balustrade, and they are hands of plaster, of wax, without a drop of blood, while below them, almost tangible with their pungent animal stench, sixteen horses and sixteen jockeys race past, bellies to the ground, the dead racing against the living, the shade of Puddu (it is him, she recognizes him!) dashing unfettered astride an elusive *bàrbero*, his white sneer turned towards her (or is she imagining it?) as he swivels to look back.

Could they be (have been?) dentures, Valeria wonders absurdly, and a hysterical laugh shakes her from head to foot, filling her eyes with tears. (It was a shock, she would say to her friend Ornella, I don't know how I kept from fainting.)

The chalky hand of Guidobaldo touches her wrist, moves up to her shoulder and settles there protectively, reassuringly.

Guidobaldo knows. Guidobaldo knew.

And Valeria ceases to tremble, accepting (she would say) the fait accompli and allowing the Palio of the Dead Contrade to run its course, interwoven with the other one, already making its breathless course towards the lethal curve of San Martino and its protective padding, the sadistic audience eager to acclaim irreparable destruction.

Now other images and fractions of images are super-imposing themselves: that first apparition of horses (six!) in the scrub amid the rain as the car climbed towards the wrong villa (two pines, two cypresses, two pines, two cypresses), and then the amazement (but wasn't it in fact dismay at first, at these two strangers who had seen what they shouldn't have seen?) of their hosts when, at dinner, she had mentioned the small pack she had glimpsed and which was already, as she thinks back, inexplicable, already essentially phantasmal. And the whole dinner with Puddu (the Last Supper, she would say to her friend Ornella), with his vulgar quips, and the tension which she had attributed to their need to secure for themselves, at all costs, the best, but also the most slippery, the most corrupt jockey of the Palio.

At all costs, thinks Valeria, shivering.

No one has fallen at the curve of San Martino, but two horses have awkwardly scraped against the mat-tresses, losing yards and yards against the others, who are already hurtling down the short slope towards the Palazzo Pubblico and then climbing eagerly towards the curve of the Casato, halved in prospect by the line of the crowd. From her balcony Valeria sees fifty thou-sand dark necks following that stretch of the track, and suddenly the whole mass turns fair, all the heads have jerked to the right, fifty thousand profiles fill the piazza. The rope is fifty yards away, the first circuit is about to end, and seven horses are leading the race.

First the Tower. Then the Eagle (and the Rooster). Then the Giraffe (and the Bear). Then the Panther (and the Viper).

Valeria accepts the contamination, the impossible osmosis, like a truth that had been predictable from the first evening.

And that's why the four (and then six) of the villa, from the very first evening, wanted her, held her there, accepted her as one of them. A woman who is generously, enthusiastically, prepared to emerge from the statistical averages, not to reject the exception, the unknown. A woman in love, who for love would be ready to...

Guidobaldo's chalky hand is still on her shoulder, and he tenses imperceptibly when she makes as if to raise her head to look at him. *Which is your, our contrada?* she is about to ask him.

But she recalls the ancient alliances, the "parties" Ascanio told her about ("even if today every *contrada* strives to win on its own account") and realizes that it doesn't matter whether Guidobaldo is for the Bear, Ranieri for the Rooster, or Elisabetta for the Oak: if Puddu wins on the horse of the Viper, all the dead *contrade* will have won with him.

"Viper," she says. "Viper!" she yells frantically, while Guidobaldo's hand once again squeezes her shoulder.

And her own scream reminds her of another one, lacerating and inhuman, in the night pregnant with silence, with scents and tattered damp clouds...

Viper, she thinks with a shiver.

XXI

Twenty seconds. Twenty-five seconds.

Ginevra's shout is repeated when the seven horses pass beneath the window in the fluid homogeneity of their gallop, and Avvocato Maggioni nods. His cool, categorizing detachment now permits him to nod, not without a touch of complacency.

That's what it was, that's how it went, he thinks, as the revelations gallop retrospectively before him. And I sensed it, I said so right from the beginning.

He nods again, unconsciously imitating the sneer of Puddu, the great cold champion who didn't fall for it, who didn't let himself get carried away (like impulsive, ingenuous Valeria) by the false starts.

Puddu is in fourth place, his knees tight against the flanks of the *bàrbero*, his squat torso glued to the mane, and he is swishing his whip with fierce determination. All the other jockeys are larger than him, including Torcicollo, because these horses (a neutral voice, well known to the lawyer, is explaining, or re-explaining) are not thoroughbreds, their size and weight are considerable, and you don't need to be a dwarf to mount them bareback but rather to have long, robust legs. Puddu's are short, but with calves, heels and thighs (and maybe other things) of steel, and it is these that have given him his numerous victories, his legendary superiority, his fame as a triumphant lover. With Elisabetta. Probably with the Filipino woman. And maybe with Ginevra too.

Ah, thinks the lawyer sorrowfully.

But the revelations are racing pell-mell: it was clear right from the start that something was wrong, from the servant with the big green umbrella, from that first offer of hospitality, from that dusty entrance hall. The four of them had not charmed him; they had never really convinced him. Not even Ginevra?

Ah, thinks Avvocato Maggioni, close to Ginevra in the yelling crowd. Thirty seconds, and the girl is leaning over the windowsill to follow Puddu's jersey, the shiny yellow-green silk of the Viper that reaches the starting line and whirls away on the second circuit.

Between the beautiful fingers that emerge from the plaster cast there has now appeared – and it seems to have slipped from inside the cast – a scarf of the same yellow-green silk, and Ginevra is waving it boldly over the piazza while she turns towards him with a smile of challenge and complicity.

Avvocato Maggioni nods at the new revelation, at the painted reptile that uncoils itself along the folds of the silk, nods at the pliable, sinuous (ah, not a gazelle, not a fawn!) little viper uncoiling by his side.

That's how it went, he thinks. That's the story.

The men and women of the villa, inconceivably involved in the larval world of the dead *contrade*, perhaps sought or summoned by those shades that had been excluded for centuries, perhaps forced, perhaps obsessed by their own maniacal ambitions, perhaps themselves infected by a spectral inconsistency – they all met up for the last "*partito*", the last funereal pact before the Palio. One for each *contrada*: the six captains, both male and female, of the suppressed *contrade*, who had long been engaged in the occult replay, in the lethal return match, the horses already chosen by lot remotely, called upon to gallop in the chiaroscuro of the scrubland and the rain, and five jockeys already summoned from the parchments of defunct city archives, retrieved from the dust of all the racetracks from the Sienese past.

Who conceived the idea of Puddu? Or maybe it was an order, carried out by the six with abject reverence and terror? To ensure that the Palio be won by one of our *contrade*, we must have the king of jockeys. But dead, of course, he too. Only after he has entered the teeming *contrada* of the departed.

And they attracted the king of jockeys with the promise of a lucrative scam; they held on to him and flattered him by dangling before his eyes the supreme double-cross, the fantastic betrayal that would set him up forever. And the cold, cynical, super-crafty Puddu fell for it, with no inkling of it as a false start.

Avvocato Maggioni sees the yellow-green jersey pass for the second time in front of the balcony of the Circolo and wonders whether Valeria sees it as well, and if she sees it, how much she has taken in, how much she has understood. Less than him, perhaps. For Valeria it is perhaps a new, thrilling development she will swallow whole, naturally, feeling no need to bother her head over it, to weigh it up. A welcome enrichment of her world already so well supplied with fantastic fruits.

Or (and yet another disentangling, yet another revelation emerges from the group) perhaps it is Valeria who actually sees more, who by sheer instinct understands more. Maybe she is the privileged one, the chosen one. It was she, after all, who made him turn into the wrong driveway, who first spotted the evanescent horses in the valley, who satisfied the last craving of the condemned bottom-biter.

What will he bite now? Valeria asks herself on her balcony, when Puddu, turning to look back, seems for the second time to direct that gleaming sneer at her.

Will his teeth clamp vainly on ectoplasmic buttocks, rarefied rear ends in the hereafter?

(And she even finds a second to wonder, with the faithful tenderness of a wife, whether her husband is seeing what she sees, whether they will be able to talk about it in the car, in bed, over a meal, to mull over this shared and astonishing experience, this "bonus souvenir" of their conjugal life.)

After all, thinks her husband, it was she who heard that nocturnal and non-human cry, though not of an owl or a mouse.

What was the biter doing out there? A rendezvous with the Filipino woman? Ah, no, thinks the lawyer, no. The rendezvous was with the little viper, who continues to wave her own symbol from the window and who on that night must have lured Puddu into the scrub with the mirage of her supple body. She was given the task of making Ganascino pass "to the other side". A genuine rite of passage, perhaps. A preordained ceremony in a circle of holm and dwarf oaks among other invisible, unspeakable presences. Yes, that's it: he approaches, spots her in the middle of the clearing, rushes forward (he doesn't know this is the last "start" of his earthly career). And she (still standing? beforehand?) winds her arms around his head (or on the ground? afterwards?), tenderly slips the silk scarf around his neck, carefully knots it and swiftly detaches herself from him. And the silk becomes animated, transforms, uncoils itself, the asp of the final *contrada* sinks its retractable teeth into the reckless man's neck. And then the cry of terror and pain, the staggering steps towards the villa, to the French window of the library, to the ash-filled hearth. And the final collapse.

That's how they must have got him, the king of jockeys, the unconquerable champion.

A chorus of enthusiastic horror greets the clash between horses and mattresses at the curve of San Martino. An animal is on the ground kicking out pitifully in an attempt to rise; it looks like a huge insect on its back, its thousand legs thrashing in the air. Beside it staggers the jockey unseated from the other *bàrbero* involved in the fall, which continues to run on its own, curiously naked and vulnerable on the tuff (if it crosses the finishing line first – says or repeats the neutral voice so familiar to the lawyer – it will have won, since even a "shaken" horse can win the Palio).

From the group of survivors (it was the Giraffe that fell, and the Bear that was unseated) the Eagle emerges in resolute bounds; it catches up with the Panther and overtakes it; but beneath the lawyer's window Torcicollo goes wild with the whip, there is a swirling exchange of blows, the Eagle resigns itself, the group has passed in a flash, it reaches the rope and clatters away for the final circuit.

All I have left is this final circuit to understand what I'm seeing, thinks the lawyer, and why I'm seeing it. A bitter revelation thrusts itself forward: the six in the villa wanted us here, my wife and me, as witnesses, in order not to be the only living people ("living"?) in this piazza, on this earth, to see this Palio of their resuscitated *contrade* being run. Every other motive – obvious, declared or hinted at over the last three days – has been a fake motive, an illusion, a pretext to keep us here. They needed us to make their phantom race real, in some way to confirm it, give it substance, remove it from the limbo of the virtual, of the purely imaginary.

Why us of all people? What do we have that's so special? Nothing. That's the very reason, in fact. Average types, averagely alive, statistically valid, chosen for our very extraneousness, our lack of involvement. Specimens, yes, but of average humanity. Chosen, when all is said and done (thinks Avvocato Maggioni), by *la sorte*, by the ironic and elaborate *sorte* of Siena.

In the remaining fifteen, twenty seconds, the lawyer meditates on his average destiny, on the probabilities that a couple like them should have stumbled into such an extraordinary adventure, and he realizes that the figures don't add up, that too many things still fail to persuade him, that the winning revelation is still concealed in the thick of the panting throng, among death and passion and Scattomints and Coca-Cola, among carabinieri, gardeners, ants, dishwashers, banners, palaces, ancient customs, X-100 tyres...

How many are there, among the tens of thousands, who can see what he sees? Only Valeria and Ginevra and her accomplices of the suppressed *contrade*? Or are there others scattered among the crowd who have been prepared by *la sorte* for this extramundane view, this vision? Or could it be all of them, because the veil between real and virtual *contrade* has miraculously dissolved, and the city (the world) is now nothing more than a homogeneous and coloured artifice?

But then (and, oh yes, a further possibility disentangles itself), but then the villa really does exert a mortal influence, a baleful, leprous, swelling irradiation that corrodes life, the meaning of life. And we have fallen into this web like passing flies, we have been sucked in by those six spiders or vampires that threaten the world... Or (a new revelation rears up) it's all been an experiment. The unfortunate Signori Maggioni are not witnesses but guinea pigs, dropped into an artificial maze to see how they will cope, how they will react to each twist, to each surprise, to each new situation, until the bursting of the fragile gland that filters the possible from the impossible...

*

Torcicollo's final sprint (the voice says neutrally) is unleashed after the curve of San Martino, when the bay horse of the Porcupine seems to be ahead by two lengths. The black horse of the Panther catches up in a few yards and at the curve of the Casato is triumphantly in first place, all by itself at fifty yards from victory.

But Avvocato Maggioni (and how many others as well?) knows, sees, that this is not the case.

Torcicollo turns round for the first time to measure the advantage he has over his pursuers, and then a second, a third time, with the quick jerk of the head that gave him his nickname. When he turns for the fourth time, terror twists his lean, bronzed face. His wide eyes confront the void, his whip slashes the air in a crazed defence against nothing.

And from nothing, from the void, his dead rival presses upon him, squeezes him, strikes him, forces him to the rope, insults him horribly with his venomous maw, drives him back into the host of pursuers that swallow him up in an instant, overtake him and leave him in the rear to eat their spurts of tuff.

Then someone wins.

But the first to pass the finishing line was the ghost *bàrbero* of the Viper, which Puddu, dropping the reins, brings to a staggering halt beneath Valeria's balcony.

XXII

Grey is the horse, and grey suddenly is the horseman at her feet, whom Valeria greets with a half-gesture; and the winner responds not with his usual sneer, but with a half-smile. Like a faint current, there passes between the two of them a sensation of obscure affinity, which ignites glimmers, faint signals, indecipherable cracklings. The scene is over.

I've left my world, Valeria will say to herself with satisfaction; for one moment I've seen the impossible (and I'll talk about it with my husband, with my friend Ornella).

They took me from my world, Puddu will say to himself bitterly, but for one impossible moment I returned to it.

This is what they must have seen, they must have understood, before retiring with sagging shoulders, fading passively into their silent backgrounds, on opposite sides of the same veil.

*

Because this is also the moment in which the veil drops from Avvocato Maggioni's eyes and the winning revelation imposes itself: obvious, sarcastic, desolate.

It is the recognition of all recognitions, the verification of all verifications.

Ah, of course. The lawyer greets it without any pleasure, without any relief.

In the swarming, crackling disentanglement of the crowd, in its incessant and raucous grisaille, in the curving frame of the palazzi around the convexity of the piazza, he finally sees the shape, the cipher that has been there before his eyes for three days: a television screen.

Ah, of course, he thinks unemotionally.

Like an electronic disturbance, he remembers thinking in the hailstorm, on seeing the colours disappear and the crystal of the car windows fill with thick transversal stripes of grey and white. He remembers the glass streaked by the pellets, like a video bombarded by crazed signals; he remembers the growling blasts of the storm, the lacerating celestial interferences.

That was undoubtedly the point – at that particular stage on the road between Arezzo and Siena – in which the phenomenon, the fatal passage, the leap into a televisual world was effected.

Ah yes. Everything is sorted out that way; everything is understood.

Three days of brisk emotions, repetitive enigmas, recurring situations, interspersed by continual commercial solicitations. Three days of old voices, old words, old storylines, hackneyed gimmicks; of pauses and returns, of gaps, interruptions, interferences, unfinished business.

And so, he asks himself with vague melancholy, is that all I've been? Not a witness nor a victim, a fly, a guinea pig, but a plain, average spectator, alongside an average wife, flipping from one channel to another, from one average programme to another?

That's all, he acknowledges dispassionately.

"So-o-o!…" sighs the American spectator with satisfaction, retrieving her binoculars but lingering at the window to follow the final sequences.

The *contrada* that thinks it has won has knocked over the barriers and is gathering beneath the tribune of the jury, spilling over the whole racetrack, forming vociferous vortexes, waves and undertows of an exuberance more ferocious than festive, mingling with the friendly and allied *contrade*, moving, wedge-like, through the crestfallen ranks of the rival *contrade*, not without a good deal of shoving, punching, spitting and frequent gestures of scorn, cold sneers and crude insults.

"Oh," exclaims the American spectator, "no-o-o!"

Torcicollo, whom the exacerbated *contradaioli* of the Panther are accusing of having deliberately lost a

Palio they had all but won, has escaped down one of the alleys that lead out of the piazza, and will spend the night in some hiding place, recounting his version to sceptical confidants.

"We-e-ell!" concludes the American woman with a final, gentle smile to Avvocato Maggioni.

Ginevra is already smiling as well, but she doesn't speak, she doesn't say anything, she doesn't propose anything. She has already taken a tiny step backwards, her hip is only brushing against his, her hands have let go of the sill, the yellow and green scarf has vanished.

"Well," says the lawyer.

The Palio has been run, the programme is over. In the great shell-shaped screen the brickwork pavement is emerging in ever broader patches, and people are gradually leaving the tribunes, balconies and merlons, the windows are black eye sockets, there are just a few figures lingering on the marbles of the Fonte Gaia, and the solitary spectator who had climbed up to the clock has descended the tower, leaving the hole in the clock face empty.

Ginevra takes another step backwards, towards the throng of guests who, after being still for so long, are clumping noisily from room to room, calling to one another, saying goodbye to one another, looking for one another.

Will Valeria come and look for me here? the lawyer asks himself mechanically. Or will she wait for me to go and look for her?

And he wonders whether she will want to go straight back to Milan ("No, listen, after all these emotions, all I want to see is my house, I'm still in a state of shock") or will she insist on following the old programme ("You'll see, a week on Paolino's farm is just what we need to get over it, it'll do us both good"). The clean break; authentic life on the ranch in touch with the earth, with nature...

When he turns round Ginevra is no longer there; for an instant, between two distant doors, amid the hubbub, he glimpses her slim, heartbreaking back and her long hair cascading over her white dress; then the fawn/madonna/kitten/viper has vanished too.

"Fine," murmurs the lawyer.

From inertia, or because there's nothing else he can do, he thinks stale thoughts: the spell is broken, the dream is over, it couldn't last, better this way. And he feels like an average rubbish bin, full of average rubbish: the old Maggioni.

When he sees that the piazza has also resigned itself to the absences, that twilight has dimmed and drained all the colours, that the television screen is blank, he goes in search of the front door, passing through three or four rooms packed with people drinking talking smoking

(Merit and Campari, Camel and Chivas Regal), he finds and descends the gloomy staircase, leaves the palazzo, sets off through the uproar of the city towards Valeria, his mind engaged in a meticulous work of replay.

The hailstorm, yes.

A crazy dislocation, an absurd, inconceivable, dimensional swerve.

And yet, in retrospect, the evidence is unassailable, sequence by sequence, scene by scene, minute by minute.

The lawyer remembers how the advertisement for the trusty X-100 tyres, which gripped the layer of icy pellets, had been imposed on his imagination; and the same image was repeated along the avenue of slime. Then the apparition of the black dog, an obvious omen of mystery and death; then the fleeting, unsettling vision of the horses in the rain. Then the ambiguous facade of the patrician villa, which opened the way for every kind of plot development: the misadventures of a large and powerful family, sadomasochistic horrors of the most depraved kind, idyllically sweet scenes among exquisite souls, or a...

Pressed up against a shop window by the swarming crowd, the lawyer finds himself face to face with a washing machine. The glassy eye stares at him.

That was why I was so wary. That was why I was suspicious.

He remembers the diffidence aroused in him by the Filipino man. He remembers Guidobaldo's mannered courtesy. He remembers, clearly, his own unease, his feeling of disorientation. And the incongruous plot twist in the dimly lit gallery, the dwarf's bite, poor Valeria's regrettable lasciviousness.

That was, he thinks as he starts walking again, surrounded by the songs of victory, jostled by the currents swirling up and down the narrow streets of Siena, that was undoubtedly the first click of the remote control, the first switch to another channel: from mystery to porn. And shortly after that, the madonna, the fairy, the impossible love story: Ginevra. Another click, this time to the scene around the fireplace, which he had compared (oh so aptly!) to an advert for a brand of whisky. Advert over, back to the earlier mystery (or another one, but basically the same), with a furtive Oriental and a secret passage, a scream in the night, a corpse in the library...

Stopping again in front of a dark shop window displaying rustic-style tables and chairs, Avvocato Maggioni mercilessly flips through all the images that have accumulated over the last three days.

Not a single one of them can be trusted. The clichéd, mannered detective story, without even a decent police officer. The apparently bureaucratic but actually downright amateur behaviour of the marshal of the carabinieri. The exaggerated Neapolitan accent of the public prosecutor, a feeble caricature. And the ridiculously directed, clumsily managed investigations, with their parade of puerile suspicions and foolish suppositions...

It was only to be expected, thinks the lawyer, that the remote control should go zapping in frantic search of something better. Except that the other channels were all just as bad. An interminable documentary on the Palio, stuffed with historical references to the Middle Ages and appropriate technical/folkloristic explanations. Have pity on us. Zap: cereals, household gadgets. Thanks so much. Zap: frustrated, lustful housewife, boring, worn-out husband, conjugal crisis, tears, scenes, futile exchange of commonplaces. For heaven's sake. Zap: shampoo and Scattomints. Zap: mad love between bourgeois woman and refined nobleman, and, simultaneously, between middle-aged lawyer and uninhibited young woman, with counter-sequences of pure soppiness and naked bodies on the bed or on the ground, quivering, gasping, gnashing, sighing. Great stuff. And the homespun western of Paolino always there in the background, with fences and foals and checked shirts and sweat-beaded brows. You can keep it. And you can keep Barabesi Cinzia's song-and-dance routines (with intermittent updates on the tennis), you can keep her Ichiko 140 and her fake grandfather's Nescafé, you can keep the pedantic weather forecasts, and the political and financial reports entrusted to that pair from Rome. You can keep it all.

Avvocato Maggioni starts walking again. The city of Siena (a well-known voice murmurs) stretches over a number of steep hills, and the differences in height between *contrada* and *contrada* are sometimes —

The lawyer stops.

My God, he thinks, I'm inside a documentary on Siena.

Raising his eyes, he sees the gothic windows of a gloomy palazzo. His shoulders brush up against the thick rings of wrought iron embedded in the facade of another historical edifice.

Avvocato Maggioni forces himself to think of Milan, of Corso di Porta Romana, of traffic lights in Via Fatebenefratelli. But the report on the post-Palio overwhelms everything; shirtless hordes come pouring in from every alleyway, the swirls and twirls of banners and scarves are back again, while chants, choruses, yells, whistles, cries and curses all raise the volume to an unbearable level.

The refuge of a grand front door reveals itself as a trap. Beyond the archway is a square courtyard, as dark as the bottom of a well, and all the windows have enormous rusty gratings. Fourteenth century? Sixteenth? A dim glow illuminates a room in one corner, forcing

Maggioni as spectator to make a choice among simultaneous programmes. Inside, there may be a damsel chained up by her uncle, or (zap) a troop of Spanish soldiers, or (zap) a young scholar bent over dusty manuscripts on his way to become Pope Piccolomini.

He must get out of here, escape from the channels. But a final glance (zap) reveals the bronze gleam of a mid-sized car, parked in the opposite corner. Fiat? BMW? Renault? Is this the purpose of the Renaissance set design?

The lawyer leaves almost at a run, and (zap) elbows and shoulders his way through the unreflecting, purely organic turmoil of the festive street. Zap. A lone man running through the unconcerned crowd in search of his wife. On his lips a name: Valeria.

Zap, thinks Avvocato Maggioni, running, escaping. He turns into a dead-end alley carved into a block of lateral night, clatters down the chipped earthenware steps, crashes into a wall, then the opposite one, pursued (zap) by assassins, by Arabian, Sicilian, Bulgarian killers. He halts, panting, at the bottom of the slope (the city of Siena is built on steep hills…) but resumes his flight when he sees, next to a rusticated doorway, a poster for (fourteenth-century?) Lines diapers.

XXIII

The area around Siena – suggests the well-known voice – is pleasant: the hills, which slope down into small valleys, are dotted with little villages (the neighbourhood of Siena is known as "Le Masse") and with numerous old villas, country houses, convents, churches, towers and artistic monuments, often unknown to tourists.

But to the eyes of Avvocato Maggioni, now leaning against a small wall that borders a deserted road, almost in the countryside now, the landscape seems somehow flattened by the darkness. No monument looms up. The scattered dots of lights do little to reveal the folds, the continual ups and downs of the terrain.

Zap? the lawyer asks himself. But nothing changes, nothing stirs; the monotonous murmuring voice finally fades into the silence.

Is only this, then, authentic? Is there no other reality but silence, the sidereal darkness?

Hey now, just a second, let's take things slowly, thinks the lawyer, who is beginning to glimpse (and he rejects it with a shiver, he strives to ward it off, to delay it) the final twist, the supreme, dazzling revelation.

But the sneeze that now shakes him seems to call forth, over there, an autobiographical and accusatory moon.

I didn't do anything, I was overwhelmed by circumstances, by statistics, by *la sorte*, the lawyer thinks, defending himself.

And yet, beyond the limpid disc, he glimpses the rims of murkier moons, like a roll of coins winding back infinitely into the past. They are fake coins, he has to admit, and it was he who forged them, not today, not after the hailstorm, but earlier, way way back.

Fake moons that irradiated schoolboy Maggioni with fakery, as he already sucked Scattomints in class, adolescent Maggioni skiing on state-of-the-art ski bindings down a snowy slope, racing on a scooter by the sea with a girl whose hair (just washed) streamed in the wind; young Maggioni dancing wildly to the pounding rhythm of some awful musical mishmash, then drooping and drooling in the season of courtship and love; Maggioni as repetitive husband and pompous father; gourmet Maggioni, discoverer of exquisite restaurants and local dishes; tourist Maggioni in Egypt, in the Seychelles; pugnacious Maggioni, asserter of original convictions on education, sport, society and philosophy; Maggioni distributor of interesting opinions on the weather, fashion, terrorism, women, the dollar, engines, whisky, the latest Nobel prize-winner, Sodoma.

What have I ever done? Maggioni asks himself, confounded in the Sienese night. What have I ever said, thought, believed?

And like that, everything is turned upside down: there has been no crossover, no leap, no impossible teleportation into a fictitious electronic universe. What he has seen in these three days is not a rough counterfeit of life but life itself. And this is the final, the definitive truth. The cipher he has been seeking all this time is zero.

Then it's not just me, he thinks, but everyone, whether they know it or not. We're all pathetically, inextricably, prisoners of this confused false bottom, of this second-rate repertoire where what has happened is soon indistinguishable from what we have merely dreamed, imagined, imitated, desired, copied, or fleetingly and erratically perceived since we were born.

The same old story, over and over again, a gigantic redubbing.

Has it always been like this, he asks himself as he is shaken by a second sneeze, for ever and ever?

What percentage of authenticity, he begins to calculate feverishly, will the Longobards, the Franks have had? Seventy-seven per cent? Ninety per cent?

And the Communes, Humanism, the Renaissance, plagues, sieges, famines, Violante of Bavaria, Duccio di Buoninsegna? All real, all authentic, like Paolino's onions? All macrobiotic?

He gives up hopelessly – who can say? Who can see anything clearly in this exponential crowd of half-shades, of half-humans, of flickering extras, of awkward body doubles who have perhaps peopled the noble *contrada* of Earth since time immemorial. All prevaricators, all forgers, myself most of all.

And he is seized by an impulse of gratitude, of nostalgia for the much-slandered villa, the magical mirror where for three days he was allowed to observe life at work, to gain an intense insight into the crass, viscous movements of reality.

It now appears to him as the most limpid, plausible, concrete place he has ever known, like a rare yolk of certainty; and its six inhabitants strike him as friends (yes, friends!) of frank, precious consistency.

They, at least, – and that's the point – belong to the *contrada* of legitimate ghosts, of cognizant spectres, and their occult race, their invisible Palio, was no more nor less than a just revenge on the rest of us, who are the real phantoms, the faded, unauthorized occupants of the *contrade* of the world.

Good for them, the lawyer thinks, silently applauding; they are a hundred per cent right.

*

The moon is cold, the air biting, and the lawyer looks in his pocket for a handkerchief to wipe his nose. His fingers encounter silk, they draw out a soft yellow-green bundle; his cheek receives a light pat.

"This corner of Siena," the omniscient Ascanio informs him, "belonged to the territory of one of the suppressed *contrade...*"

They are all around him, the bland, insinuating, irresistible winners. Ascanio in all his leanness, Elisabetta in her long-fringed shawl, G.baldo with his lunar, dickhead face, the pair from Rome, dark and standing slightly apart. And Ginevra, who now sits down on the low wall beside him and takes his arm.

"Did *you* put it in my pocket?"

"Yes."

"Do you want me to put it around my neck?"

"Yes."

Well, hang on just a second, average lawyer Maggioni thinks, hesitating.

This, he reflects, would be a real clean break. He imagines Paolino among his jams, he imagines Valeria, who will probably end up hiding out there herself, working on her vaporous transformations among the flies.

Going back to his pocket, his average hand meets the packet of Scattomints and pulls it out to face the moon, the universe.

But by now, after the Palio of the Dead Contrade, after the Palio of the Revelations, there is something or someone in him (maybe his own shadow picked out by the moon on the ancient stones of Siena) that feels a vast disinterest, an overflowing incompatibility with the *contrada* of Scattomints, that knows it can no longer live there.

Maybe it is his own shadow that speaks for him while his hand drops the packet without any regret over the wall.

"Why don't you put it on me?"

Ginevra folds and refolds the scarf until it is a slender, languid strip, and tenderly wraps the silk viper around the neck of Avvocato Maggioni, a smiling, consenting ghost.